Hazel Green

ALSO BY ODO HIRSCH

for children
Antonio S and the Mystery of Theodore Guzman
Hazel Green
Bartlett and the Ice Voyage
Something's Fishy, Hazel Green!
Bartlett and the City of Flames
Frankel Mouse
Bartlett and the Forest of Plenty

for adults
Yoss

ODO HIRSCH was born in Australia, where he studied medicine and worked as a doctor. He is now a busines strategy consultant based in London. His award-winning books for children are favourites with young and old, and have been translated into several languages.

ANDREW McLEAN grew up in a country town in Victoria, and now lives in Melbourne. He is an illustrator and artist, with paintings in major galleries around Australia. His work includes many well-loved picture books, including the *Josh* series and *Make It I'm the Mother*, written by his wife Janet.

for Diana

First published in 1999 by
Allen & Unwin Pty Ltd
83 Alexander Street
Crows Nest NSW 2065
Australia

Phone: (61 2) 8425 0100
Fax: (61 2) 9906 2218
E-mail: info@allenandunwin.com
Web: www.allenandunwin.com

National Library of Australia
Cataloguing-in-Publication entry:
Hirsch, Odo.
Hazel Green.
ISBN 1 86448 961 8.
I. Title.
A823.3

Set in 11.5pt Granjon
Cover and text designed and typeset by Ruth Grüner
Cover illustrations by Andrew McLean
Printed in Australia by McPherson's Printing Group

7 9 10 8

Hazel Green

Odo Hirsch

Illustrations by Andrew McLean

ALLEN & UNWIN

1

Hazel Green looked down from her balcony. It was only six o'clock, but that was the best time of the day, because hardly anyone else was awake. Far below, the street was empty. There was barely a sound.

A bird twittered. It must have been on top of one of the other apartment buildings, or perhaps perched on a window ledge. Hazel listened. The bird sang again. Its voice was as clear as water, as pure as the light from the sun that was rising over the buildings around her. The air was still chilly from the night. Hazel pulled her dressing-gown snug around her. The tiles under her bare feet were cold. If her mother had been awake she would have told her to put her slippers on. But Hazel's mother wasn't awake, and neither was her father. And the chilly air made her skin tingle, and the chirping song of the bird made her smile, and the empty street made her happy, because everything she could see from the balcony on the twelfth floor, the whole city, was *hers*, and there wasn't anyone else to share it with.

Suddenly a man appeared on the pavement below.

He had a big belly with a white apron tied around it. His head was bald. From above, where Hazel was watching him, he looked just like a round dumpling with a cherry on top. He stopped and stretched out his arms. He threw back his head and warmed his face in the sunlight. He had a thick black moustache, just like a walrus. Like a big salty walrus, thought Hazel, who had swum out of the sea and waddled through the city and decided that here, in this particular street, would be a very good place to stop and stretch his flippers and throw back his head and feel the wonderful warmth of the sunlight . . .

'Hazel!'

The man had opened his eyes. There was a big grin on his face.

'Hazel Green!'

Hazel waved.

'You don't want to sleep?' he shouted, his voice booming all the way up the side of the building.

Hazel shook her head.

The man frowned, as if wondering why a girl would not want to sleep when it was still so early. But he always frowned, whenever he looked up to find Hazel Green on her balcony early in the morning. And then he would always shout: 'Well, what are you waiting for? Come down, Hazel Green!'

Hazel skipped down the stairs, all twelve flights of them. The man was waiting for her on the pavement.

'No slippers?' he said, looking at her bare feet.

'Slippers are for Flippers, Mr Volio,' said Hazel Green.

Mr Volio frowned. 'Slippers are for Flippers. What does that mean, Hazel?'

It didn't mean anything. Why should it? Hazel had just made it up.

Mr Volio shook his head. 'Where do you learn these things, at school? When I went to school we didn't learn such things. We learned—'

'How to bake!'

'No, Hazel,' said Mr Volio seriously, shaking his head. 'I learned how to bake *after* I went to school. Of course, I didn't go to school for very long, because—'

'They *wouldn't* teach you how to bake!'

Mr Volio laughed. 'Where do you learn these things, Hazel Green? Where?'

Hazel didn't say. Not at school, that was for sure. You don't learn everything at school.

'Come on,' said Mr Volio, 'let's find something good for you to eat.'

Hazel thought that was an excellent idea. She had been getting hungrier and hungrier while Mr Volio had decided to have his conversation about Slippers and Flippers, which was only to be expected, because just where they were standing there was a particularly delicious smell in the air, which would have made anyone hungry even if it wasn't six o'clock in the morning and time for an early breakfast. It was a warm, buttery smell, with raisins and sugar and flour in it, delicious crispy crusts in it, cinnamon buns in it, sesame seeds in it, and . . . in short, the smell of a bakery that has been working all night to make shelf loads of fresh pastries and basketfuls of breads. And the reason for this, quite simply, was that they just happened to be standing right in front of a bakery that *had* been working all night, which belonged to Mr Volio, who just happened to be a baker, a very fine baker, perhaps the best in the city.

Mr Murray, of course, would not have agreed. He was a baker as well, and his shop was around the corner from Mr Volio's, on another side of Hazel Green's apartment building. The whole ground floor of the building was taken up by shops of one sort or another, so you never had far to go if you needed anything. Mr Murray, in his own way, was also a very fine baker, and there were always long arguments in the elevators about who was the best. But in reality there was no comparison. Mr Murray's special skill was in breads, especially breads with lots of seeds, and of course his famous pumpernickels. Some people came from right across the city for his pumpernickel loaves. Mr Volio, on the other hand, was a pastry wizard, and the cakes he made melted in your mouth. Yet those who supported Mr Volio never went to Mr Murray for their bread, while those who favoured Mr Murray never stepped foot inside Mr Volio's shop for their cakes . . . well, almost never, because no one could resist Mr Volio's cherry strudel for their *whole* life!

For the children of the building, of course, the decision was easy—pastries were much nicer than breads, and besides, since Mr Volio was always inventing new cakes, he was always looking for people to sample his latest recipes. But better than that, he couldn't resist giving samples of older recipes either! You only had to walk in and Mr Volio, slapping his belly or twirling his moustache, would call out to Elizabeth, the lady who served behind the counter, to give you a cake. Mr Murray, on the other hand, was thin and bony, and no one got a sample in his shop, not even of the pumpernickel bread which was supposed to be so famous.

But Hazel Green was no ordinary sampler. No one else ever came down so early in the morning. No one else was ever allowed behind the shop into the bakery itself, warm and rich with the smells of ingredients and cooking. There, Hazel knew, amongst ovens, vats, sacks of flour and barrels of cream, the bakers would now be sitting, tired out after a whole night's work. There she would find the two Mrs Volios, Mr Volio's mother and his wife, who made the quiches and pies. There she would find the kneader, Andrew McAndrew, whose father's name had also been Andrew, resting the powerful muscles of his arms after hours of kneading dough for the breads. There she would find Martin, the pastry chef, who shared all of Mr Volio's most important secrets and worked with him to create his greatest recipes. And there she would find the four apprentices, who prepared the dough and whipped the cream and oiled the trays and washed the tins and did all the other things that an apprentice has to do when learning to be a baker, just as Mr Volio himself had been an apprentice when he left school because they wouldn't teach him to bake.

Now, at six o'clock in the morning, before anyone else was up, it was already the end of their day. They would all be sitting around the kneading table, faces flushed in the warmth, sipping mugs of cocoa, surrounded by the products of their labour, baskets of fresh breads, trays of pastries, pallets of pies. Only Martin would still be working, using the last heat of the ovens, after all the breads had been baked, to produce his most delicate pastries, concentrating so hard as he worked that you could have shouted in his ear and he would barely have heard.

2

Old Mrs Volio, the baker's mother, gave Hazel a cup of cocoa.

'Now, what would you like?' she asked.

Hazel looked around the bakery. She hardly wasted a second on the breads. The pastries were laid out on trays stacked high in steel frames. Vanilla slices, chocolate éclairs, almond croissants, strawberry tarts, custard

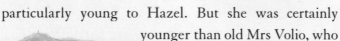

doughnuts, raspberry crunches, ginger fingers . . . Hazel's belly began to rumble.

'What about a lovely chocolate rollo?' said young Mrs Volio, the baker's wife. Everyone called her young Mrs Volio, although she didn't look particularly young to Hazel. But she was certainly younger than old Mrs Volio, who was definitely old. Old Mrs Volio must have been almost a hundred!

Young Mrs Volio picked up

a rich brown pastry with a delicious nubbin of chocolate showing through the end.

Yes, thought Hazel, a lovely chocolate rollo, fresh from the oven, with warm runny chocolate that would flood into your mouth and roll, roll, *rollo* down your tongue as soon as you took a bite . . .'

'No, Teresa,' said Mr Volio.

'No?'

Mr Volio shook his head. He was grinning mischievously. Then he winked.

'Eh, Teresa?'

Mrs Volio grinned as well. Hazel didn't know what they were talking about. The baker went over to a tray in the corner. Unlike the other trays, it was covered with a cloth. He reached under the cloth and took a pastry out. He handled it as carefully as if it were made of glass. Everyone in the bakery had turned to watch, the two Mrs Volios, and Andrew McAndrew, and the four apprentices, who were all sitting in a row on the other side of the table—everyone except Martin, the pastry chef, who was working with the last heat of the ovens, lost in concentration.

Mr Volio put the pastry in Hazel's hand. 'Now you tell me, Hazel, whether Mr Murray has ever made something like *this*!'

Hazel was holding a round pastry with a shortbread crust. The top was made out of toffee, and a glazed strawberry sat in the middle. She examined it carefully. She had never seen anything like it before. It must have been Mr Volio's latest invention.

Hazel took a bite. First the sweet toffee fractured between her teeth. Then she tasted a wonderful smooth caramel custard. Then there were swirls of strawberry. Then there was a delicious surge of almond and cinnamon. And then, just when she thought she had discovered all the flavours in the pastry, her tongue dipped into a layer of chocolate covering the base. And all in one bite!

Hazel looked up. Even Martin had turned away from the oven and was watching her. 'No,' she said.

Mr Volio's eyes almost popped out of his head. 'No? What do you mean, no?'

'No, Mr Murray has never made anything like *this*.'

Mr Volio stared at her for a moment. Then he laughed. He slapped his forehead with his broad palm, leaving a big patch of flour. 'Oh, Hazel. You had me worried.' He shook his finger. 'You had me worried, Hazel Green.'

Everyone laughed except the apprentices. They sat on the other side of the table and glared at Hazel. The apprentices always glared. It was as if that were part of their job: whip the cream, make the dough and glare at people.

'What's it called?' said Hazel, when she had swallowed the last mouthful of Mr Volio's scrumptious new invention.

'Well that's just the problem,' said Andrew McAndrew, putting down his cocoa and crossing his arms. 'We're not sure.'

'Strawberry Delight,' muttered one of the apprentices.

'Chocolate Surprise,' growled another.

'No, no,' said Mr Volio, 'that's the kind of name Mr Murray would think of. We have to do better than that.'

'Custard Supreme, that's what *I* would call it,' said Andrew McAndrew.

Hazel frowned. She looked back at the tray, where the rest of the pastries were hidden by the cloth. The thing that made this invention really special, she thought, was all the layers of flavours, and then the chocolate at the bottom. The way it was just waiting for you when you thought there was nothing else to find. But Mr Volio was right, 'Chocolate Surprise' wasn't special enough. And neither was 'Custard Supreme'. The name had to be better than that.

Suddenly she had an idea.

'Chocolate Dipper.'

'Chocolate *Dipper*?' said Mr Volio. 'Chocolate Dipper,'

he murmured, as if trying it out for himself. 'Martin. *Martin!* Chocolate Dipper, that's Hazel's suggestion.'

Martin, who had turned back to the oven again, looked over his shoulder. Everyone watched to see his response. He thought for a moment, then he nodded.

'Chocolate Dipper!' Mr Volio repeated excitedly, shaking his finger at the apprentices. 'You see, why couldn't you think of that? Four of you! And you couldn't figure out a name that one girl could think of! What use are you? Do you think baking is just about kneading and folding? No. *Naming!* It's about naming as well.'

The apprentices glanced sheepishly at Mr Volio.

'Get up. All of you. Go and take a Chocolate Dipper, and while you're eating it, think of how to work out its name!'

The apprentices got up. One after another they went over to the cloth-covered tray and took a Chocolate Dipper. They still looked as miserable as ever, but they weren't really unhappy. In fact, they enjoyed Mr Volio's punishments, which always involved eating a pastry.

'Now we've got such a good name, it's certain to be a success,' said Mr Volio, turning back to Hazel. He lowered his voice. 'You see, Hazel, we're not going to sell it until Frogg Day. Martin and I have just been perfecting it.'

'Well, I think it's perfect now,' said Hazel.

'Yes, but we're going to keep it a secret until then. It will be the best Frogg Day ever. Everyone will remember it as the day Mr Volio revealed his Chocolate Dipper.'

Everyone? Maybe not *everyone*, thought Hazel.

'*Bakers* will remember it like that, Stephen,' said young Mrs Volio.

'Bakers, of course bakers will. But not only bakers!' cried Mr Volio, and then he clapped his hand over his mouth, suddenly remembering to lower his voice. By now he had flour all over his face. 'You mustn't tell anybody, Hazel. Not a word. All right? If Mr Murray got his hands on this recipe . . .'

Hazel nodded. Did Mr Volio really think she needed to be told?

'Do you really think Hazel needs to be told, Stephen?' said young Mrs Volio.

Mr Volio smiled foolishly.

'Anyway, Mr Murray couldn't make Chocolate Dippers like you and Martin,' said Hazel.

Mr Volio grinned. 'That's true, isn't it, Martin?'

Martin didn't hear. He was loading a tray of especially delicate meringues and had no time for anything else.

Hazel stood up to go. Her parents would be awake soon.

'Haven't you got any slippers?' said old Mrs Volio, noticing Hazel's bare feet for the first time.

Mr Volio winked at Hazel. 'Mama, Slippers are for Flippers.'

'Who don't like Chocolate Dippers,' added Hazel, winking back at Mr Volio.

'Where does she learn these things, where?' cried old Mrs Volio, shaking her head.

'You watch,' said Mr Volio, 'on Frogg Day she'll be marching without any shoes. Right, Hazel?'

Hazel stopped. She had never marched on Frogg Day before. She had never seen *any* children marching on Frogg Day.

'All the children from the building used to march on Frogg Day,' said Mr Volio.

'When?' said Hazel.

Mr Volio thought. 'A long time ago,' he said.

'It must be twenty years ago now' said old Mrs Volio, 'maybe more.'

Hazel frowned. 'Why don't they march now?'

'Too frightened,' said the biggest apprentice, sniggering.

'Too scared,' said another.

'*Who's* too scared?' demanded Hazel.

The biggest apprentice shrugged. 'Ask yourself. Twenty years ago they used to march: girls no older than you, Hazel Green.'

'That's enough!' said Mr Volio. 'Who are you to talk? Couldn't even think of a name for a cake!'

'Neither could you,' muttered the apprentice, secretly

hoping that Mr Volio would make him eat another Chocolate Dipper as punishment.

Mr Volio pretended he didn't hear. If he punished his apprentices every time they were rude to him, there would never be anything left to sell.

'Don't worry about him, Hazel,' said young Mrs Volio. 'Do you want something else before you go?'

Hazel shook her head: she wouldn't have room for breakfast when she got back upstairs!

Mr Volio let Hazel out of the shop. The street was still empty. There was still a chill in the air. The pavement under her bare feet was cold.

But Hazel didn't go back upstairs at once. After Mr Volio left her, she lingered on the deserted sidewalk, thinking.

Too scared? Who was scared?

Hazel thought about all the Frogg Day marches she had seen: the colours and noise and excitement. The crowds were so thick you could barely slip through them to get to the front. When you did get to the front, there was the parade: marching bands and banners and floats, winding its way past as you watched. And until today, it had never occurred to Hazel that anything was missing.

But something *was* missing, something important.

Children marching on Frogg Day? And *why* not?

3

Frogg Day was the most important day in the city. Visitors from abroad, especially those who couldn't spell, often wondered why the city made such a fuss over slimy little animals who jumped around. But it wasn't about frogs at all. It was about Victor Frogg, who had been the city's mayor, and then a senator, and eventually the prime minister in the terrible days of the Silk Wars, when the country almost broke apart. It was Victor Frogg who had brought peace again, and Union Day was proclaimed to celebrate it. On Union Day there were marches in every city, but none was more spectacular than the march in the town where Victor Frogg had been born, where they called it Frogg Day instead.

The march was always led by Victor Frogg's granddaughter, who led it very slowly, because she was very old, but refused to be driven in a car. Behind her came the government representatives, and then there was always a special contingent from Hazel Green's apartment building, which held such an important place in the march for one simple reason: it was here, more than one hundred years earlier, that Victor Frogg had been born.

He was born in a corner apartment on the

sixth floor, and there was a plaque on the wall just beside the door to remind everybody about it. A lady called Mrs Kaspowitz lived in the apartment now, together with her son, Sergio, who worked as a polisher for one of the silver-smiths in the city. Mrs Kaspowitz was not particularly pleased about the fact that Victor Frogg was born there. It was not that Mrs Kaspowitz wished that Victor Frogg had never been born—*no one* could have wished that—it was just that she wished it could have happened somewhere else. People were always coming to see the apartment, and she had to give them cups of tea and biscuits. 'A room's just a room,' she would say, trying to discourage the people who knocked at her door, 'there's nothing to see'. But people never believed her, and she always had to let them in. Sometimes she showed them Sergio's bedroom, saying that Victor Frogg was born there, and sometimes she showed them the dining room, and occasionally, if she was very irritated, she showed them the broom cupboard, explaining that Victor Frogg's mother had been a very unusual woman who enjoyed small rooms with little light. Of course, Mrs Kaspowitz had no idea which room Victor Frogg had been born in, and she would probably have denied that he had been born there at all if not for the plaque that the council had decided to put up.

Hazel Green knew all of this, and she herself had often been in Mrs Kaspowitz's apartment to look for the place where Victor Frogg was born. But children marching on Frogg Day? Hazel had never heard about *that* before.

'It's true,' said Mrs Gluck, who had the flower shop on the ground floor. 'Children did march on Frogg Day, now that you mention it.'

'When?' asked Hazel.

Mrs Gluck frowned. She gazed thoughtfully at the bouquet she was making. Her hands didn't stop moving for an instant, as if they could make the bouquet all by themselves while she tried to remember.

'I bet she doesn't know,' whispered a boy who was sitting next to Hazel. His name was Marcus Bunn. He wore spectacles with gold frames and his cheeks were always shiny and red, as if he had just come in out of the snow. Marcus Bunn was always running after Hazel, although he would never have admitted that he liked coming with her to visit Mrs Gluck's flower shop, which was no place for a *boy*. But he probably wouldn't have admitted that he liked Hazel Green, either, even though he liked her more than any other girl, much more than his sister, and, in fact, more than anyone else at all.

Hazel Green didn't reply. Of course Mrs Gluck knew.

Mrs Gluck knew everything about every celebration, party, event, spectacle and occasion in the town, because she arranged the flowers for them. Marcus was just being ridiculous again.

'About twenty years ago,' said Mrs Gluck.

'Why?' said Hazel.

'Why not?' said Mrs Gluck. She finished the bouquet, whipping a length of twine around the stems. It was a beautiful arrangement with yellow roses and cream-coloured tulips. Mrs Gluck held it out for Hazel to see. 'It's for one of my oldest customers,' she said. 'His daughter is eighteen today.'

'And is *that* all she's getting?' demanded Marcus Bunn, pulling a face.

Mrs Gluck laughed. 'I'm not sure, Marcus. I can see you wouldn't be very happy if you got this for your birthday.'

'No, I wouldn't be very happy, Mrs Gluck. I'd be pretty mad.'

'You're already mad,' said Hazel Green.

'Well, I'd be even madder,' said Marcus, puffing out his red cheeks to show just how mad a boy could get if he got flowers for his birthday.

Mrs Gluck put the bouquet in a vase. She had silky grey hair that was gathered in a bun, and her dress was made out of a grey material covered in flowers. But there weren't as many kinds of flowers on Mrs Gluck's dress as there were in the room where they were sitting! This was Mrs Gluck's workroom at the back of her shop, where she made up all the arrangements and decorations that people ordered while her assistant served customers in the front. The colours of a thousand blooms flared around them, yellow, blue, red, purple, green, orange, pink, white and all the shades in between. There were bouquets that Mrs Gluck had already made and thick bunches of flowers that she would soon use. All the space on the floor, every inch on the shelves, was taken up with brightly filled vases, buckets and tubs of water. And in the middle, where they sat, was the big worktable, strewn with leaves and cut-off stems, lengths of twine and spools of ribbon, clipping scissors and puddles of water that had dripped from the flowers as Mrs Gluck worked. The air was rich with perfume, and the room was always cool so that the flowers wouldn't wilt.

Mrs Gluck stopped to check her list of orders. Then she went to the vases around the room, gathering flowers for the next bouquet. This time she collected purple-tipped spears of irises, and crinkly lemon-coloured carnations, and a pair of yellow rose buds that were as small and delicate and perfect as a baby's hands. No one ever told Mrs Gluck what to put in her bouquets. They only needed to tell her what the occasion was, and Mrs Gluck would know exactly which flowers were right.

Soon the new arrangement was taking shape. Marcus Bunn forgot he was uninterested and stared with his mouth open. Mrs Gluck's quick hands combined the colours and shapes of flower, stem and leaf. She brought them together in a way which made them look as if they had never been apart.

'It must be at least twenty years,' said Mrs Gluck, thinking about the Frogg Day march again. 'But there was a time when the children of the Moodey Building were always in the march. It wouldn't have been complete without them.'

'Why not?' said Hazel.

'Well, Victor Frogg was born here. He grew up here, just like you, Hazel. So if *anyone* should represent him, it's the children. Just think: if you were born in the Moodey Building and grew up to be a great leader, who would you want to represent the Moodey Building: the adults or the children?'

'The children,' said Hazel. 'Adults don't know anything about what it's like to grow up.'

'Nothing,' added Marcus, shaking his head.

'Well, there you are,' said Mrs Gluck, and Hazel didn't know whether she was agreeing with her, or talking about the bouquet, which she had just finished.

Mrs Gluck looked at her order list again.

'Why did they stop marching?' asked Hazel.

'The children?' Mrs Gluck stopped to think. 'I don't know.'

'Could they march again?'

'I suppose so,' said Mrs Gluck. She went around the room, collecting flowers. 'Yes, I suppose so, if they wanted to.'

Marcus glanced inquisitively at Hazel. He hadn't heard about *this* before! But a moment later he was watching Mrs Gluck again, fascinated by her quick, skilful hands, which seemed to know exactly where to place each stem and flower.

'Come on,' said Hazel, 'let's go.'

Marcus looked up with a start.

'You don't want to watch Mrs Gluck arrange *flowers*, do you?'

'Of course not,' spluttered Marcus, although he had already turned back to her again, eager to see how she was going to use the huge, bright orange bloom that she had in her hand.

'Well, come on, then,' said Hazel.

They got up.

'Goodbye, Mrs Gluck.'

'Goodbye, Hazel.'

'Goodbye, Mrs Gluck. I only came to keep Hazel company.'

'Goodbye, Marcus. Do you know where this flower is going to go?'

'No.'

'Here!' said Mrs Gluck, and she placed the big orange flower, which was as big as your palm and was called a gerbera, in the very centre of the bouquet, where it became a bright, smiling orange heart, lighting up every other flower around it.

Mrs Gluck laughed. Marcus was still staring while Hazel dragged him away.

Outside, Marcus was back to his usual self, pretending that Mrs Gluck's flower shop was no place for a boy. 'I just don't see the point of flowers. Just because they're pretty: ten minutes after you've got them, they're already dead.'

'They're not *pretty*,' said Hazel.

'Of course they're pretty. Every time my father gets flowers for my mother, she says, "Oh, how pretty!" Just like that. *Every* time she gets them.'

Hazel stopped. 'They might be pretty, but that's not the point, Marcus.'

Marcus gazed at her silently. He pushed his spectacles up his nose. When Hazel used that tone of voice, it was better not to argue with her.

'Well, what is the point?' he asked very quietly.

'It's what they mean,' said Hazel.

'And what do they mean?'

Hazel shook her head. 'That depends, doesn't it? They can say anything, and in the most beautiful way, like a poem.'

Mrs Gluck knew the meaning of every single flower. Sometimes, when Hazel came to sit with her in her workroom, she would tell her. Of course, there were books about how to arrange flowers, and there were even rules that people had made up, like never putting a lily with a rose unless there's a daffodil to separate them. Mrs Gluck laughed at those. *Rules* were only good for people who couldn't tell, in their hearts, what to do. She would explain why she chose a particular flower for a particular place, and why she put an arrangement together in a certain way, rule or no rule, and when she had finished, Hazel could see that the bouquet was exactly as Mrs Gluck had described, and said exactly what she wanted it to say, but in a way that was more beautiful than any words that a person could have chosen.

Marcus was still waiting. There were lots of people on the street, rushing past them. They were standing outside the fishmonger's shop. Both of them liked going into the fishmonger's shop. They liked looking at the tank where the lobsters crawled over each other, snapping their claws. They liked looking at the brown, horny shells of the crabs, and the smooth, dark shells of the mussels, and the orange prawns with their wispy antennae and lines of legs, and the rows of shiny fish that lay glistening on ice. They liked watching Mr Petrusca, the fishmonger, take a fish in one of his thick, red hands, and a knife in the other, and slit, gut and fillet it under the cold water of the tap. Well, Hazel liked watching that, and Marcus pretended that he did.

Hazel looked in through the window. Someone had just bought a big mackerel, and Mr Petrusca was lifting it off the ice. Already his other hand was reaching for the knife.

'Come on, let's go and watch Mr Petrusca for a while,' said Hazel.

4

Not everyone thought they should march on Frogg Day. There was a lot of discussion each morning as the children from the Moodey Building set out for school, which was three blocks away .

'Who wants to march for a *frog?*' said Robert Fischer, and he leapt around the pavement, waving his arms like an orang-utan.

Hazel watched Robert Fischer jumping ahead of them. His satchel flipped up and down on his back. With a bit of luck it would knock him in the back of the head.

'Ow!' cried Robert as it hit him.

Robert would make a very good orang-utan, thought Hazel. He had long arms, just like the orang-utans she had seen in pictures. Only his hair wasn't the right colour. He would have to dye it red. Anyway, what Robert said didn't matter. He always listened to Leon Davis, who was good at football and was growing so fast that he needed new shoes every three months. Lots of people listened to Leon Davis, almost as many as listened to Hazel herself. Whenever anything had to be decided, it was always Leon against her.

The last time, for instance, was during the summer, on the annual Moodey Building Picnic.

Everyone always went on the summer picnic. The food was certain to be good, because the shopkeepers from the ground floor brought the most delicious pieces from their stores. Mr and Mrs Coughlin, the fruiterers, always brought ten huge watermelons and split them open with their flat knives. The picnic was beside the river, at Billet's Point, where there was a waterfall and the river opened out into a deep pool surrounded by the drooping branches of willows. After everyone had eaten and the adults were all falling asleep, or sitting around under the trees, the question was: what sort of competition should they have? Leon Davis wanted swimming races, because he was the strongest boy there and could do the butterfly better than anyone. A diving competition, said Hazel, from the top of the waterfall. Diving's for girls, said Leon Davis, glancing at the waterfall. You're scared of the height, said Hazel, who was a bit scared of it herself, but would jump from the top if Leon Davis would. Leon Davis wouldn't. Hazel ran to the top and dared him to follow. Quite a few of the others came with her. Leon tried to organise a swimming competition with those who were left. As soon as they set off for the first race Hazel took a deep breath, closed her eyes, and jumped right into the middle of them.

As she hit the water she sent up an enormous splash that drenched one of the elderly ladies who was snoozing on the river bank. She missed Paul Boone, who was coming third in the race, by about four inches. Paul gulped a whole mouthful of water in surprise. The race came to a halt. Paul Boone started hitting her. Some of the others jumped as well, and Marcus Bunn said he *would* have jumped but there was no one to hold his spectacles. Then there was a big fight in the water between the jumpers and the racers which lasted until the fathers waded in and started pulling children out, claiming that someone would get drowned. It was Mr Volio who pulled Hazel away from Leon, but she still managed to get one last kick at him as he dragged her out of the water.

Of course, that kind of thing wouldn't do on Frogg Day. The whole city would be watching. It would be no good having Robert Fischer, for instance, charging around like an orang-utan, knocking people over with his waving arms, or Leon Davis throwing eggs from one of the windows in revenge for the summer picnic. Everyone had to agree, or they could forget the whole idea.

Hazel could see that Leon Davis was thinking about it. For a few days he didn't say anything, and Robert Fischer clowned around on the pavement, making fun of frogs and tadpoles and people who want to march for them. This time, Hazel didn't accuse Leon of being scared. She let others do the talking: Hamish Rae, for instance, who loved parades and exhibitions and anything where there was lots of noise, or Mandy Furstow, whose father was a composer and had written the 'Silkman's March', which the bands always played on Frogg Day. There was nothing Mandy wanted to do more than march in time with her father's music. She and Hamish walked on either side of Leon Davis and between them they thought of every reason, argument and explanation to prove that the children of the Moodey Building should march. Then they thought of a few more. By the time they were finished, Leon Davis knew more reasons to march than Hazel Green could have *ever* thought of.

But still he didn't speak. Hazel stopped him one day, just after everyone had come back from school. They went to the alley behind the apartment building, where the huge steel rubbish containers were kept. Rubbish Alley always had a moist, foul smell, and no one ever went there. It was the best place for a private talk.

'Well?' said Hazel.

'Well, what?' said Leon. He glanced at her suspiciously.

Hazel grinned. Leon Davis was playing dumb. 'Yes or no, Leon?'

Still Leon Davis pretended he didn't know what she was talking about. He looked down at his shoes, which were almost too small for him again. Then he kicked an old, rotting apple that had fallen out of one of the rubbish containers.

'I know what your problem is,' said Hazel.

'What problem?'

'You didn't think of it yourself.'

'Think of what?'

'That's it, isn't it?' Hazel watched Leon's face. 'You didn't think of it yourself and you just don't want to admit it's a good idea.'

'That's rubbish, Hazel.'

'No, it's not. It's perfectly true.'

'It isn't.'

'Swear it isn't true, then. Swear on your nose!'

'No. That's stupid.'

Hazel stared at him silently. It *was* stupid. It made no more sense to swear on your nose than to swear on your elbow, or your little toe, for that matter. But everyone did it, and Leon was no exception. It was the biggest test, the most solemn oath, and no one dared to misuse it. In the end, if you weren't prepared to put your finger on your nose and swear, none of the Moodey children would believe you.

'Swear! On your nose!'

'No!'

'Then I know I'm right.'

Leon didn't say anything.

'You know, Leon, you can't have *all* the good ideas,' said Hazel in her friendliest tone, even though she would have liked to see him come up with *one* occasionally.

'I didn't say it was because it was your idea,' said Leon Davis.

'Oh? Really? Then why did you say—'

'I *didn't* say.'

'Well, if you ask me, Leon Davis—'

'I *didn't* ask you, Hazel Green!'

They were standing very close to one another. They were staring fiercely into each other's eyes. If either of them had made the slightest move they would have been at each other in a flash, continuing the fight that had started in the water at Billet's Point. But this time there would have been no Mr Volio to separate them. And then there would have been *no* chance of marching on Frogg Day.

'All right,' said Hazel quietly. After a moment she stepped away. She went to the edge of the alley and leaned against the wall. 'I'll just wait until you *do* say.'

Leon Davis looked around for something else to kick. There was a blackened banana skin that lay squashed flat on the ground, but that was no good. It would have stuck to his shoe. There were some bits of paper—they were even less use. Eventually he kicked one of the bits of the apple that he had kicked before.

He turned to Hazel. 'All right, here's the deal: we'll organise it together. You won't do anything I don't agree with, and I won't do anything you don't agree with. When we march, we'll both march together at the front. Neither one ahead of the other.'

Hazel hadn't even thought about where she would march. 'You can march in front, it doesn't bother me.'

'No. Together. In the front.'

Hazel shrugged.

'Swear on your nose!'

'I thought you said that was stupid,' said Hazel.

'Swear on your *nose*, Hazel Green!'

Hazel put her finger on her nose. 'What about you?'

Leon Davis put his finger on his nose as well. They watched each other carefully. Then, at exactly the same instant, as if they both knew precisely when the other was going to say it, they opened their mouths.

'I swear . . .'

The next day, when Robert Fischer jumped around on the pavement like an orang-utan, Leon Davis told him to stop. It was a shame, thought Hazel, because Robert's jumping was definitely getting better, and he really might have turned into an ape if he kept practising.

Everyone else stopped as well. Other children walked past them on their way to school, wondering why everyone from the Moodey Building was just standing around. Maybe they had decided to go on strike. Going on strike from school was a very popular idea but no one had yet had the courage to try it.

'We think we should march on Frogg Day,' announced Hazel Green.

'Who's *we*?' demanded Robert Fisher, and he waved his arms orang-utanishly.

'Everyone,' said Hazel.

'Well, I don't!' retorted Robert.

'I do,' said Leon Davis. 'I agree with Hazel. And anyone who doesn't agree is just too proud to admit it's a good idea which she thought of first.'

Robert Fischer was gazing at Leon in disbelief. His hands hung limply by his sides. 'Are you sure we should march?' he murmured.

'Yes,' said Leon.

'All right,' said Robert, and suddenly he went jumping away again, crying out, 'We'll march like Froggs!' until his satchel hit him in the back of the head.

5

Being willing to march on Frogg Day wasn't the end of the matter—it was only the beginning. You couldn't just turn up on the day. Somehow you had to get a place in the procession. And if you were from the Moodey Building, you had to get into the Moodey contingent.

'It's Mr Winkel you want to see,' Mrs Gluck told Hazel, 'he always organises the Moodey delegation.'

Hazel poked out her tongue. 'Mr Winkel!'

Mrs Gluck nodded. 'He's the one to see.'

Mr Winkel sold leather goods. His shop was on the same side of the building as Mr Murray's bakery, with the Frengel delicatessen on one side of it and Mrs Lundy's hat shop on the other. Everyone knew the window of Mr Winkel's shop. It had briefcases and handbags, and whole sets of wallets and matching keycases, but that wasn't why it was famous: looming over everything was an enormous leather saddle with gleaming stirrups hanging from its straps. It was the colour of ox blood, and you could just imagine a huge fiery horse rearing beneath it. The saddle had been there for years, and not once had anyone even asked its price. But Mr Winkel kept it right in the middle of the window, always perfectly polished and beautifully oiled, dwarfing every other piece on show, as if to say that his shop was a *real* leather goods store, where a person could get everything, from the smallest keycase to the biggest saddle.

But the only people who ever went into Mr Winkel's shop were old, much too old to be riding horses, and Mr Winkel himself certainly didn't encourage any youngsters.

Marcus Bunn warned Hazel to be very careful. He said he would be waiting just outside Mr Winkel's shop in case she needed his help. But Hazel wasn't relying on him. Marcus never did anything with the slightest risk unless he could find someone to hold his spectacles first, so unless there was someone *else* waiting with him he wasn't going to run into Mr Winkel's shop to rescue her. But it was nice that he did offer, because Mr Winkel's shop really was quite a scary place. Of course, Hazel had never been inside, but it was just a feeling she had.

She pushed hesitantly on the door. As they had agreed in Rubbish Alley, Leon Davis was with her.

There was a thick smell of leather. That was the first thing Hazel noticed. The next thing was that the light inside the shop was very dim. Everything seemed brown. The third thing she noticed was the leather goods: shelves and shelves of briefcases, handbags and portfolios covering the walls. And the fourth thing was Mr Winkel. But *he* had already noticed them.

'Yes?' he said, in a tone that sounded more as if he were saying no.

He was standing behind his counter. He was not a very big man, but he was very bald, with a big, bony nose and bushy eyebrows that made him look like an eagle. His piercing brown eyes were as sharp as an eagle as well. Hazel couldn't see his hands, and for a second she wondered whether he had an eagle's talons instead of fingers.

Hazel stopped. Leon had stopped half a pace behind her. The door had closed.

'Can I help you?' said Mr Winkel, in a tone that sounded as if he were saying that he couldn't.

'Maybe,' said Hazel.

Mr Winkel's bushy eyebrows rose. He glanced towards the corner of the shop. Hazel followed his gaze. There was someone else sitting on a stool. It was Mr McCulloch, the barber!

'You haven't come to buy a leather good, have you?' asked Mr Winkel.

Hazel shook her head.

'And you haven't come to find out the time, I hope,' said Mr Winkel, 'because I don't sell time, not in this shop.'

Hazel shook her head.

'And you?' said Mr Winkel, glancing at Leon.

Leon shook his head as well.

'Well, then, it's probably time you left. You're interrupting us.'

'We didn't mean to interrupt,' said Hazel. She glanced at Mr McCulloch. What was *he* doing here? He had a very stern expression on his face. Hazel didn't know that Mr McCulloch's expression could be so stern. Every boy in the building had his hair cut by him.

Suddenly Mr McCulloch winked at Hazel. But the expression on his face didn't change for a second.

'I said, you're interrupting us.'

Hazel looked back at Mr Winkel. His bushy eyebrows had risen again, as if he were so astonished to see that the two children were still in his shop that he didn't know what to think.

'The Frogg March!' Hazel said suddenly.

Mr Winkel's expression changed. His eyebrows dropped low over his eyes, and he peered fiercely into Hazel's face.

'How do you know?'

'How do I know what?' said Hazel.

'That's what we were talking about when you interrupted us.'

'Oh,' said Hazel. 'That's what everyone's talking about.'

Mr Winkel didn't look convinced.

'In fact, that's why we're here.'

Mr Winkel gazed at Hazel for a moment. He rubbed his chin. There weren't any talons there, just fingers.

'Explain, little girl.'

Hazel looked around to see which *little* girl he was talking to.

'Explain, please.'

'Me?'

Mr Winkel glared impatiently.

'Well, it's quite simple, Mr Winkel. We're here to march.'

'Really? Simple, is it? And when do you want to march, right now?'

Hazel laughed. 'Not now, Mr Winkel! On Frogg Day, of course.'

'Oh, I see. On *Frogg* Day.' Mr Winkel glanced at Mr McCulloch, to see whether he had ever come across such an insolent child. But Mr McCulloch didn't say a word. He looked as if he were having quite enough trouble just maintaining his stern expression.

'*I* know who you are,' said Mr Winkel, suddenly turning back to Hazel. 'You're Hazel Green, aren't you?'

'Yes,' said Hazel, who didn't see why she should deny it. 'And this is Leon Davis.'

'Hello,' whispered Leon.

'Well, I don't know what you're talking about,' said Mr Winkel. 'Someone has put a very strange idea into your head, little girl.'

'It was Mr Volio, actually.'

'And Mrs Coughlin,' murmured Leon.

'And Mrs Gluck.'

'Was it?' inquired Mr Winkel. 'Was it really?'

'Yes,' said Hazel. 'A long time ago, children from the Moodey Building used to march on Frogg Day. Not everyone knows this, Mr Winkel. I didn't know it myself until a week ago. But it's true. And it's also quite important, because Victor Frogg was born in the Moodey Building and this is where he grew up. And so if anyone should march, it's the children. That's what Mrs Gluck says and I agree.'

Mr Winkel stared at Hazel Green, speechless. His eyebrows had climbed half way up his head, and this time they were almost frozen there in astonishment.

A chuckle broke out in the corner.

Mr Winkel spun and fixed Mr McCulloch with his most piercing look. The barber sucked in his lips and tried to put his stern expression back on his face.

'Impossible!' Mr Winkel said curtly, turning back to Hazel.

'No, Mr Winkel, it's absolutely true.'

'I know it's *true*!' Mr Winkel was looking quite angry now. 'But that was then and this is now.'

'And now is now and tomorrow will be the day after,' said Hazel, who knew all about that kind of thing.

This time Mr McCulloch burst out laughing and not even Mr Winkel's glare could stop him.

'Hazel Green, you are quite as rude as I've heard!' cried Mr Winkel, while Mr McCulloch almost fell off the stool.

Hazel didn't know what this meant, because she had no idea what Mr Winkel had been told.

'Children don't march on Frogg Day,' he said, as if that were that.

'They did,' said Hazel.

'That was years ago. Twenty years ago. Before *I* became head of the organising committee.'

'Mr Winkel,' said Hazel, 'when did you become head of the organising committee?'

'Twenty years ago.'

Hazel nodded. She was beginning to understand. 'Mr Winkel,' she said, 'does it say anywhere that children can't march?'

Mr Winkel didn't answer.

'I mean, twenty years ago, when children stopped

marching, there must have been a rule or something. Wasn't there? I mean, it wasn't as if someone just stopped them marching, or discouraged them, or told them to stop *interrrrrupting*?'

'Hazel Green, you are the *most*—'

'Arthur,' said Mr McCulloch suddenly, 'the children *did* march.'

'I know, but—'

'And people *did* think it was a very nice idea. They used to quite like it, as I remember.'

'Yes, but—'

'And it doesn't *say* anywhere that they can't.'

'No, but—'

'Or even that they *shouldn't*. Does it?'

'No,' Mr Winkel threw up his arms. 'No, but—'

'But what?'

'But children are always trouble, that's what! And you, little girl,' said Mr Winkel, waving his finger at Hazel, 'are the proof. Children have no place in parades. They just create difficulties.'

'Pigeons have no place in parades either!' replied Hazel.

Mr Winkel frowned. What did she mean? Mr McCulloch frowned as well, and so did Leon Davis. Hazel crossed her arms and put a very knowing look on her face. She had no idea what it meant, she had just made it up.

'Arthur,' said Mr McCulloch eventually, winking at Hazel, 'you wouldn't want anybody to think the organising committee wasn't completely fair. We wouldn't want it said we discouraged people from taking part.'

Mr Winkel's fingers tapped on the glass top of his counter.

'Arthur?'

'You can't just *march*, you know,' he said suddenly to Hazel.

Why couldn't she just march?

'Oh, no,' said Mr Winkel, smiling menacingly and looking very much like an eagle again. 'You have to have a display, something interesting and exciting, to show your respect for the memory of Victor Frogg. That's just what Mr McCulloch and I were discussing when you interrupted us: this year's float for the Moodey Building.'

'Well, that's all right then, isn't it?' said Hazel, since Mr Winkel had apparently solved the problem for her. 'We'll use your float. We're from the Moodey Building as well, you know.'

Mr Winkel shook his head, making a tutting noise with his tongue. 'No no no. If the children want to march, well, they must have a separate display, something of their own. Am I right, Bert? I'm just trying to make sure we're being *fair*.'

Mr McCulloch folded his arms and thought. Hazel

watched him, wondering what he would say. Eventually he nodded.

'All right,' said Hazel, shrugging, 'we'll make a display.'

'Good,' said Mr Winkel, as if that pleased him very much. 'And you'll have to make a design first, so we can be sure it's appropriate. And we need to make sure it's safe, of course.'

'All right,' said Hazel, 'we'll make a design first.'

'Good,' said Mr Winkel. 'Just bring me the design when it's ready.'

'All right,' said Leon Davis, who had suddenly decided it was safe to open his mouth, and he turned to go.

But Hazel didn't follow him immediately. 'One more thing, Mr Winkel. When we bring the design, Mr McCulloch will look at it as well, won't he?'

Mr McCulloch grinned. Mr Winkel's bushy eyebrows dropped low in a fierce scowl. Suddenly he looked like the angriest eagle that had ever flown into a leather goods shop.

6

To listen to Leon Davis, you would have thought it was *he* who had convinced the terrifying Mr Winkel to let them march in the parade. There stood Mr Winkel . . . behind his counter . . . with yellow teeth and cruel, bloodshot eyes that could have frozen a leopard in its spots, gripping the glass and shaking it in his rage. Who would dare to stand up to him? Who wouldn't melt like ice and dribble out of the shop under the door? Only he, Leon Davis, had the courage to speak: clear, calm, without the slightest fear, there, in the dark den behind the ox-blood saddle, where no child had spoken before. How Mr Winkel shivered and shook! How his shoulders heaved and his fists clenched! But Mr Winkel, at last, had met his match. Finally, here was a boy who would not turn and run. Here was a boy who—

'Leon, that's rubbish,' said Hazel, who was quite annoyed to have found him talking like that. There were four boys standing around Leon Davis, and every one of them was staring at him with his mouth wide open. Robert Fischer's mouth was so wide open that Hazel could see the little pink thing that hung down at the back of his tongue, which was not only annoying, but disgusting. 'Why don't you tell them the truth?' she demanded.

'I *am* telling them the truth,' said Leon.

'Well, it's a very unusual truth,' said Hazel. 'It's really the same as a lie, isn't it?'

Leon didn't answer. The other boys were still watching him. They would have believed anything he said, no matter how ridiculous it was.

'Well, then, Mr Davis, what did *I* do?' said Hazel. 'I suppose I just hid behind you, in case the terrifying Mr Winkel breathed fire in my face?'

Robert Fischer sniggered. Hazel punched him on the arm.

'Ow!' said Robert.

'Watch out Fischer Pischer, because I'm much more terrifying than Mr Winkel any day!'

Robert Fischer jumped away and stood at a safe distance, glowering at Hazel.

'*Boo!*' said Hazel, and Robert Fischer jumped again.

She turned back to Leon. 'Well?'

'Well what?'

'Have we got a design?'

'I thought *you* were making the design.'

'Did you? And what about doing everything together? What about that?'

Leon Davis glanced nervously at the other boys. Obviously, he hadn't told them about the deal in Rubbish Alley. He had probably told them he was in charge and Hazel would have to do whatever he said.

Things were never going to work like this!

'Courtyard!' said Hazel.

'Courtyard?'

Hazel nodded.

'When?' said Leon.

'This Saturday. Ten o'clock.'

'No good. I've got football.'

'All right. Three o'clock.'

Leon nodded. Hazel looked at the others. 'You tell everybody: Courtyard. This Saturday. Three o'clock.'

At three o'clock on Saturday afternoon there were seventeen people in the courtyard of the Moodey Building. They stood in two groups, one around Hazel, and the other group around Leon.

'Does everyone here want to march?' said Hazel. 'Because we need a design.'

The faces around her were blank.

Now Leon spoke. 'We need a display. That's the deal.'

'We need to have something to show our respect for Victor Frogg,' explained Hazel. 'A float. That's the deal we made with Mr Winkel. We make a float—we get to march.' Hazel looked around. 'Any ideas?'

'A float?' said Maurice Tobbler, scratching his head. Everyone called him Cobbler, because it rhymed with Tobbler, and because he always took such a long time to consider everything. 'A float?' he said again, still thinking.

'A float, Cobbler!' everyone shouted.

'All right. I was only thinking.'

'*I* know!' said Mandy, 'We need something on wheels.'

'Wheels?' said Cobbler. 'Hmmmm, you might be right. Wheels . . .'

'What kind of wheels?' someone said.

'Big wheels!'

'*Which* wheels?'

'Car wheels!' . . . 'Motorbike wheels!' . . . 'Steering wheels!' . . . 'Bicycle wheels!' . . . 'Cartwheels!'

'*Cartwheels?*' shouted Hazel, trying to make herself heard.

'I can do cartwheels!' cried Susie Bunn, who was the youngest there.

'She can, you know,' said Marcus, beaming with pride. But he didn't need to tell them, because Susie was already cartwheeling away across the courtyard: four, five, six cartwheels in a row. Then she came skipping back, and she threw in a somersault just for fun.

'Cartwheels?' said Hazel. 'Does anyone have a cart?'

People shook their heads. Who would have a cart in an apartment?

'I do,' said Robert Fischer. 'We use it to get from the bedroom to the kitchen. It saves so much walking.'

'Very funny. Really, does anyone have a cart? Or something like a cart?'

'A cart?' said Cobbler. 'Hmmm. Now, a cart isn't something—'

'A cart, Cobbler!' everyone cried. 'Yes or no?'

'Well, yes.'

'*Yes?*'

'And no.'

Now *nobody* understood.

'It's not really a cart, but it's like a cart.'

'Cobbler, what are you talking about?'

'It's a barrow.'

A barrow? What was a barrow? Not even Abby Simpkin, who always got top marks for English, could say. Everyone looked at her and she started to blush.

'A barrow' said Cobbler, in a tone that was very solemn and self-important, because it was not often that he knew a word that Abby Simpkin had never heard of—in fact, it had never happened before—'is like a cart that you push.'

'A handcart!' said Abby.

'*Like* a handcart,' Cobbler said, holding a finger in the air, just in case Abby should get the idea that she *had* known what a barrow was.

'Well, where is this barrow, Cobbler?' said Hazel. 'Let's see it.'

'Oh, I don't have it. It's in my uncle's garage. I've seen it there lots of times.'

'What's it doing there?'

Cobbler hesitated. He chewed his lip for a moment. 'He used to sell apples and pumpkins from it in the market.'

There were shouts of laughter all around. *'Apples and Pumpkins! Pumpkins and Apples!'*

'Cobbler, I thought your uncle played the French horn in the orchestra,' said Mandy Furstow quietly.

'That's my other uncle,' muttered Cobbler, and he scratched his head again sheepishly. Cobbler's hair was just a blond fuzz, because his mother took him to Mr McCulloch every two weeks and made the barber cut his hair so short you could barely see it.

'Apples and Pumpkins! Pumpkins and Apples!'

'There's nothing wrong with that,' said Hazel Green.

'Anyway,' said Cobbler, 'he doesn't use it anymore. Now he sells uniforms to the police and the fire brigade.'

'And what about fire helmets? Does he sell them as well?' asked Robert Fischer.

'Of course,' said Cobbler.

No one laughed at that.

'Do you think we can use it?' said Hazel. Everyone else

seemed to have forgotten what they had been talking about in the first place.

'What?'

'The barrow, Cobbler.'

'Maybe.' Cobbler thought. 'It's got wheels. That's what we wanted, isn't it?'

True, that's what they wanted.

'We'll have to push it, obviously,' said Leon Davis.

What sort of a display was that? Mr Winkel demanded something interesting and exciting. A bunch of children pushing a handcart? They'd look like they'd got mixed up in the procession on the way back from the market!

'I'll stand on it,' said Robert Fischer, beating his chest. 'And I'll wear my cape!'

Excellent, thought Hazel. That would make all the difference.

'Well, we could put something on it,' said Mandy Furstow.

'Like what?'

'Like . . . boxes. Or crates. We could get some crates from Mr and Mrs Coughlin. They've always got too many. We could build something on top of the barrow. And we could paint the boxes, and make it look nice, and put streamers on it. Streamers that will blow in the wind.'

But what would they build?

There was silence. Cobbler frowned, scratching the

fuzz on his head. The others thought as well. Everyone stared at something: the ground, the wall, a window, a weed, trying to work it out. What should they build? Hazel looked right up to the top of the building, squinting in the sunlight, wondering.

Then she knew. It was right in front of her!

'The Moodey Building.'

The others looked at her.

'The Moodey Building! We'll build it out of crates, and we'll paint them to look like the building. We'll build it on the barrow. It'll be perfect! Can't you imagine it?' Hazel could, she could see it as if the parade were right in front of her eyes. 'Look: there's old Miss Frogg, and now here come all the boring old government people marching behind her, but now, already, you can see something new, an enormous building moving towards you in the distance, towering over everything else. What is it? For a while you don't recognise it, then suddenly you do: the Moodey Building, where Victor Frogg was born! And when it gets closer you see the children of the Moodey Building all around it, marching in his honour!'

'And I'll be sitting on top,' said Robert Fischer, 'wearing my cape!'

It wasn't hard to work out the design. Cobbler took Hazel and Leon to his uncle's garage to measure the barrow. It was 2.3 metres long and 1.2 metres wide, with

a pair of long handles at the back, and it had two thick tyres in the middle and a fold-down support at either end to hold it up when no one was pushing it. Then they went back and carefully looked at the Moodey Building from every side to make sure they got the dimensions and the features exactly right. They made a list of all the shops around the three sides of the building, and they counted the windows, and they measured the entrance, and they checked Rubbish Alley to see what the building looked like from that angle. Then Mandy Furstow drew the design, because she was very good at sketching and knew how to make something look solid on the page instead of flat. The building would be 5.4 metres tall, and Leon Davis wanted it to be even taller, but then the dimensions wouldn't have been right. Besides, they would already need to get quite a lot of fruit crates from the Coughlins just to make it that big.

Wait until we show *this* to Mr Winkel, Hazel thought when Mandy had finished the drawing. Not only was there a picture of the float, but each measurement was clearly marked on it, and they had written 'Cobbler's Barrow' underneath, so no one could say there was anything they hadn't thought of. On the way to school everyone wanted to see it, and everyone wanted to see it again on the way back. It was brilliant, everyone agreed, absolutely brilliant.

'Of course, it will fall,' said a voice.

Hazel stopped in mid-sentence. She looked around. She was standing on the pavement with the drawing in her hands, explaining all the measurements to Hamish Rae and Alli Reddick.

The voice belonged to Yakov Plonsk, and he was looking at the design over her shoulder.

'It will fall,' said Yakov Plonsk again. He smiled contemptuously at Hazel, and then he walked away.

Hazel stared, open-mouthed. Hamish Rae grabbed the design. 'It's just the Yak, he wants everything to fall!' he cried, and he ran off with Alli Reddick to show the drawing to somebody else.

Hazel didn't chase him. She was still staring. Yakov Plonsk was walking briskly away from her. As usual, he was by himself. Soon he would turn into the Moodey Building and disappear.

Would it fall?

In the distance, Yakov Plonsk was walking faster and faster. Hazel began to run.

But she didn't reach him. Just when she was getting close, Mr Murray stepped out of his bakery and caught her arm.

7

'Hello, Hazel,' said Mr Murray. He held up a chocolate éclair with his free hand and dangled it in front of her nose. 'Come inside.'

Come inside? Hazel squirmed and struggled, keeping her eyes on Yakov Plonsk. But Mr Murray held on to her. Yakov Plonsk turned the corner and disappeared. It was no use now, she'd never catch him.

'That's better. Come inside, Hazel.' Mr Murray dangled the éclair again. He peered at her expectantly. The sharp Adam's apple in his throat bobbed up and down. Hazel sniffed, shook off Mr Murray's grasp and went inside. He could keep his stale old éclair for himself!

Mr Murray's shop had a big mirror that ran right along the wall behind the counter. Along one of the other walls were the shelves for the breads, including one whole section for the famous pumpernickels. Now, at the end of the day, the shelves were mostly empty. A few pumpernickels remained for customers who would rush in after work.

There was only one lady serving behind the counter. Mr Murray gave her the éclair as they went past, heading for the door to the bakery. Suddenly Hazel wheeled around and went back to the middle of the counter. Mr

Murray turned and ran after her. Hazel stared silently at the trays behind the glass. The lady behind the counter waited for her to speak, but Hazel didn't say anything. It was fun just to watch Mr Murray flapping around her like a big crawky crow.

'What? What do you want, Hazel? Is it the strawberry tart? The fruit slice?'

Hazel didn't say anything.

'The toffee crunch? The prune pie?'

Hazel screwed up her nose. *The prune pie?*

'What? What is it?' Mr Murray glanced desperately at the lady behind the counter. 'The cinnamon scone? The—'

'The custard tart?' said the lady.

'Yes,' said Hazel, 'the custard tart.'

'Why *didn't* you say so?' cried Mr Murray, prancing behind the counter on his long, thin legs, and flapping his quick, thin arms, and bumping the lady aside with his sharp, thin hip before she had time to get anywhere near the tray of custard tarts. He grabbed three in each hand. 'How many?'

'Just one,' said Hazel.

Mr Murray dumped five tarts on the startled lady and dashed back to Hazel. He slapped a single custard tart in her hand.

'Now, come on,' he said impatiently, and set off again past his pumpernickel breads.

The bakery was quiet. In another hour or two everyone would arrive for the night's work. The oven would be lit. Aprons would be tied. Then pots would clang, doors slam, voices shout, trays clatter, water would gush out of the taps, dough would slap on the table, the air would fill with a white mist of flour and the oven, swallowing load after load of bread, would flood the bakery with its rising, glowing heat.

But now the bakery was cool. The wood of the kneading table was bare. The steel of the pots gleamed as if they had never been used. There was only one apprentice there, sitting far down towards the end of the bakery, cutting up fruit for pies. There was a great pile of peaches, pears, apricots and apples in front of him, and he wearily skinned, sliced and slit one piece of fruit after another.

The apprentice glanced up as Hazel and Mr Murray came in. Like his master, he was thin and lanky. He continued to chop lazily, hardly even bothering to look at the knife. The fruit was coming out in all shapes and sizes. Normally Mr Murray would have picked up an apple and thrown it at him to help him concentrate, but Mr Murray had other things on his mind, and so did the apprentice, who seemed a lot more interested in the conversation that Mr Murray was about to have with Hazel than in the pies that were going to be baked later that night.

Hazel sat down beside the kneading table. She dipped her tongue into the custard tart. It wasn't bad. The custard had a vanilla flavour with a hint of something else. Nutmeg, perhaps. Actually, it was really quite good—for Mr Murray. She let its taste dissolve gradually in her mouth.

'Good?' said Mr Murray, who had perched himself on the edge of the table and was watching her closely.

Hazel shrugged. Mr Murray ought to know by now whether his own custard was any good! She took another dollop, as if she needed another taste to be sure. Then she bit some of the crust, which was made out of thick shortbread. Oh, no, the crust wasn't as good as the custard. You couldn't compare it to the crusts that Mr Volio and Martin produced. Why was that? Why was it that one baker was good at pastry crusts and another was good at breads? Why couldn't you be good at both? Maybe there was some kind of rule. Hazel almost laughed out loud. A Baker's Rule! You can be good at one but not the other: take your choice. Which one would *she* choose? Hazel took another bite of the tart, trying to make up her mind. No, she *wouldn't* choose! She would be just like Mrs Gluck—other people could follow the rules, *she* would be good at both. That would show them! *If* she chose to be a baker, of course, like Mr Volio or Mr Murray . . . who was still sitting on the corner of the kneading table in front of her, she suddenly remembered, having forgotten all about him.

He'd better hurry up if he wants to say something, thought Hazel, glancing at the custard tart in her hand. She'd go when she finished it, she decided, whether Mr Murray had said what he wanted or not. And she took another bite, as if telling him to get a move on.

Mr Murray coughed, clearing his throat.

Hazel took another nibble. He didn't have much time.

'Hazel . . .' said Mr Murray, peering craftily at her.

Hazel waited. It was amazing how often people just said your name and expected you to respond, as if they were telling you something you didn't know already.

'I understand you were . . .' Mr Murray paused for a moment, and when he continued his voice was no more than a whisper, 'that you were . . . that is . . . *in Mr Volio's bakery.*'

Hazel gazed blankly at Mr Murray. Then she glanced at the apprentice, who was leaning forward with his knife poised in the air, straining to hear.

Mr Murray looked around as well. This time he did pick up an apple and threw it at the apprentice. 'Cut!' he shouted. 'Cut, Sebastian!'

The apprentice picked up a peach and cut. But it

wouldn't be long before he was straining to hear again.

'Well?' said Mr Murray.

'Of course I've been in Mr Volio's bakery,' said Hazel. 'I've been there millions of times. I'm sure you already know that, Mr Murray.'

'I don't mean those other times.'

'Well, which time *do* you mean?' said Hazel, and she took another dollop of the custard with her tongue.

'The . . . *other* time,' said Mr Murray slyly.

'Which other time?' said Hazel.

Mr Murray jumped to his feet in exasperation. 'The other time! The other time!' he shouted, flapping his arms about. 'Do I have to spell it out?'

Yes, thought Hazel, you do.

'Cut, Sebastian!' shouted Mr Murray, and this time he threw two apples, one after the other, at the apprentice. The first one hit him on the knee, and the second one sailed over his head, because Sebastian had immediately fallen to the ground, writhing with his long legs.

'Look, let's not play games, Hazel Green. You know which time I'm talking about. One morning, very early. Not more than two weeks ago.'

How did Mr Murray know about *that*?

Mr Murray sat down on the table again. 'I can see we understand each other,' he said.

Hazel hoped not.

'Now tell me, Hazel,' said Mr Murray, in his most oily voice, the kind of voice that he probably thought would make a child trust him, 'what did you see there that day?'

'In Mr Volio's bakery?'

Mr Murray nodded.

Sebastian, who had given up writhing and climbed back on his stool, leaned further forward that ever.

Hazel smiled. 'Cakes.'

'Cakes?'

'And pastries.'

'*Pastries?*' Mr Murray's eyes were wide, his mouth was open, as if he were ready to pounce and devour in one gulp the *pastries* that Hazel had seen in Mr Volio's bakery.

'Yes,' said Hazel.

Mr Murray frowned. 'And? *And?*'

'And that's what I saw,' said Hazel.

'Can't you be a little bit more . . . specific?'

'It was a long time ago,' said Hazel.

'No, it wasn't!

Not even two weeks ago. That's not a long time! That's hardly *any* time.'

That depends, thought Hazel. It's a long time if you're a banana.

'Would you like another custard tart, Hazel?' said Mr Murray, using his sickly-sweet voice again.

'I haven't finished this one.'

'Something else, then? A butternut Napoleon?'

Hazel looked around the bakery. She caught Sebastian's eye. Sebastian screwed up his nose and poked his tongue out. He was slicing an apple. He'd slice his own finger if he wasn't careful, thought Hazel.

'Hazel Green!' said Mr Murray suddenly. He hissed like a snake. 'I know you were in Mr Volio's. I know he has a new pastry. And I know you tried it!'

'Ow!' shouted Sebastian.

Hazel grinned as Sebastian sucked his cut finger. Mr Murray ignored him.

'Well?'

'You seem to know everything already, Mr Murray,' said Hazel. 'Why ask me?'

Mr Murray smiled. He looked as if he just swallowed something very bitter. 'I don't know *everything*,' he said.

Well, of course, no one could know *everything*. That was obvious.

'For instance, I don't know *what* it was that you tried. It might have been a new kind of éclair, mightn't it?' Mr Murray paused, peering very closely at Hazel's face. 'Or it might have been a strudel.' Mr Murray paused again. 'A tart? . . . A pie? . . . A crumble? You don't actually have to say, you know. You could just nod, if you like. Why don't you just nod when I'm right?'

'I don't think you're right.'

'No, wait until I mention a pastry.'

'No, I don't think you're right to ask. Besides, even if I did taste a new pastry at Mr Volio's, how do you know about it?'

'Don't you worry about that, Hazel. That isn't important.'

'Isn't it?'

'No,' said Mr Murray, and he patted Hazel on the head, as if she were just a little girl who shouldn't worry about the things that grown-ups do. Sebastian laughed silently and pulled a face, which just made Hazel even madder.

Hazel stood up. 'I'm going, Mr Murray.'

'But Hazel, we haven't finished our talk.'

They *had* finished their talk. Mr Murray just didn't realise it.

'If you want to know what pastries Mr Volio has, why don't you ask *him*?' said Hazel, and she popped the last piece of custard tart in her mouth.

'Hazel Green, come back here!'

Hazel skipped out of the bakery. Did Mr Murray really think she would tell him about Mr Volio's new invention? The idea was ridiculous. It was so ridiculous that she laughed out loud as she left the shop, and the lady behind the counter, thinking that Mr Murray must have told her something very funny, smiled in return.

No, Mr Murray would have to find someone else if he wanted information like that—and there was no one else to give it to him. Hazel had more important things on her mind. Just what had the Yak meant when he said their display of the Moodey Building would fall?

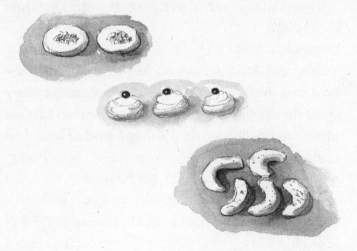

8

Who was the Yak? Where had he come from? Where was he going? No one knew. He had appeared suddenly in the Moodey Building about a year earlier. There was a mother, a father and the Yak himself. No brothers or sisters. He hardly talked to anyone, and when he did speak there was an accent to show that he came from somewhere else. Another country, probably. But where? Russia? Finland? Mozambique? The Yak didn't say, and no one could tell.

Actually, he didn't look much like a yak, although Hazel didn't find this out until it was too late—because it was *she* who had thought of the name, and no sooner had she said it than everyone was using it. But yaks are hairy, and the Yak always had his hair cut very neat and short. And yaks have long faces, and the Yak had quite a pointy face with a sharp chin. And of course yaks have four legs, and the Yak only had two—but Hazel knew *that* from the beginning. It was only the part about the hair and the face that she didn't find out until later, when Abby Simpkin told her, but by then everyone was calling out 'Yak, Yak' after the strange, silent boy called Yakov who always walked home from school alone, and it was too late to change it.

It was only the Yak who thought there was something

wrong with the Moodey Building display.

Everyone else loved it. Mandy Furstow had drawn it so well that you only had to glance at the design to visualise it. She had even drawn Robert Fischer sitting on the top, wearing a top hat as well as his cape. Cobbler's uncle agreed to lend them his barrow as soon as he saw it. The Coughlins were already storing fruit crates for them in the back of their shop. Mrs Steene, who owned the art supplies store, got so excited that she promised them paints, brushes and streamers on the spot, even though she hardly ever gave anything away. And as for Mr Winkel, not even he could find a reason to refuse. He tried, of course, examining the design with a look of grave doubt under his bushy eyebrows. But Hazel made sure that Mr McCulloch was there as well, and when Mr McCulloch said, 'Well, Arthur, it looks fine to me', Mr Winkel couldn't do anything but shake his head and say that it looked fine to him as well, although the tone of his voice sounded as if there were something that wasn't fine about it, not fine at all.

But the Yak disagreed. Hamish Rae and Alli Reddick, who had heard him as well, couldn't care less. Hazel wasn't so sure. The Yak, after all, did not speak so often that one should necessarily ignore him when he did. And he was clever. No one ever beat him in maths, and only Abby Simpkin ever beat him in English. And English was the Yak's *second* language. If he was that good at English, he must be a whiz at Russian or Finnish or Mozambiquan, or whatever it was that he did speak.

Would it fall? Would it really fall? Mr Winkel didn't say so, and he would have seized any reason to stop them marching. But maybe the Yak knew something that no one else, not even Mr Winkel, could know.

There was only one way to find out.

Hazel Green had never been inside the apartment where the Yak lived. The apartment was on the third floor, and before his family moved in it had been occupied by an old man called Mr Nevver.

Mr Nevver, who had lived all by himself, used to come out twice a day, once in the morning to buy bread rolls from Mr Volio and once in the afternoon to drink coffee in the *Vienna* café on the corner. In the winter he sat inside at the third table from the door and in the

summer he sat outside under the awning, and he always sat with two friends who were just as old as himself and came from other buildings in the street. 'And he *Nevver* goes out apart from that,' the children would whisper to one another whenever they saw him shuffling back from the café, 'and he *Nevver* drinks coffee anywhere but the *Vienna*,' they would say, beginning to giggle, 'and he *Nevvver* drinks it with anyone but his two friends,' they would conclude, unable to keep their laughter quiet by now, even if Mr Nevver was close enough to hear them. But Mr Nevver never looked around to see what they were laughing at, because he already knew, and he never grew angry or shouted at them to stop—because it is an odd thing to be called Nevver, and even odder if your first name is Horace, and it was already eighty years that people had been making jokes and giggling about his name, and fifty years since he had stopped worrying about it, and now that he was old, Horace Nevver actually enjoyed the idea that he could still give children some fun—and it nevver made him unhappy, even if it was only his name that they found so amusing.

The door to the Yak's apartment was like all the other doors in the building, made of thick wood and painted a rich, deep green, with a brass knocker in the middle. But Hazel hesitated in front of it.

She didn't really *want* to knock. It had already taken her a few days just to make up her mind to go there. For one thing, she didn't think the Yak would want to talk to her. He didn't seem to like *anybody*. And for another thing, she couldn't help feeling guilty. After all, calling him the Yak was her idea, but it wasn't really a very nice idea, when you stopped to think about it. And she *hadn't* stopped to think about it, that was the problem. It just jumped straight out of her mouth as soon as she heard the name of the new boy in the building, and suddenly everybody was using it. But Yaks, when all was said and done, were hairy beasts. They probably had fleas. According to the encyclopaedia, people used them to carry heavy loads in the mountains of Tibet. Hazel didn't think *she* would like to be known as a hairy, load-carrying beast with Tibetan fleas. Why should the Yak like it? And if people did call her that, she didn't think she would be very happy with the person who started the whole thing. She'd probably punch him on the nose.

Hazel stared at the door, wondering if the Yak knew who had made up his name and whether he was much of a puncher.

Eventually she knocked. The sound resounded in the corridor.

A woman opened the door. It was the Yak's mother. She was slim and tall, and her golden-coloured hair made her look even taller, because it swirled around and behind and up above her head like a seashell. She wore a silk gown the colour of emerald, and her fingernails were painted emerald as well. Her shoes were amber. She was holding a silver brooch in one hand, as if she had just been about to put it on when Hazel knocked. She didn't look like any other mother Hazel had ever seen.

'Yes?' said the Yak's mother.

'Is the Y—is Yakov in?' said Hazel.

'Yakov?' said the Yak's mother. She had the same accent as her son, but it was stronger.

Hazel nodded.

The Yak's mother shrugged. 'I suppose so,' she said. 'He's never out.'

Hazel grinned, thinking this was a joke, but the Yak's mother didn't smile.

'I'm Hazel. Hazel Green.'

'Really?'

Hazel nodded. The Yak's mother continued to gaze at her. Perhaps *she* knew that Hazel had made up her son's name. When you thought about it, being a Yak's mother wasn't much better than being a Yak. In fact, it amounted to the same thing!

'I'm sorry,' said Hazel.

'What for?'

'For . . .' Hazel paused, wondering whether the Yak's mother knew. Suddenly a thought flashed through her mind: *Never admit something unless you have to.* She couldn't remember who had told her that. Maybe she had made it up herself. She could tell there must be something wrong with it, but now wasn't the time to work out what it was! 'For . . . disturbing you.'

'You haven't disturbed me,' said the Yak's mother. She glanced at the brooch in her hand and clasped her emerald-ended fingers around it. 'Why, does it look as if you have disturbed me?'

Hazel frowned. 'Do you think Yakov would mind seeing me, Mrs Plonsk?'

'I don't know. You would have to ask Yakov.'

They both thought about that for a moment. No, it wouldn't work, because Hazel would have to see him first in order to ask him.

'Why don't *I* ask him?' said the Yak's mother.

Hazel thought that would be a very good idea.

'Come in, then,' she said, and closed the door behind Hazel.

Hazel waited in the hallway. The Yak's apartment had furniture everywhere. In the hallway alone there was a lamp, a table, a coat stand, a small desk, a set of bookshelves, two chairs, a shoe rack, a porcelain vase, a potted plant, a magazine holder, a grandfather clock and an enormous urn for umbrellas, not to mention the oil

paintings on the walls and the Persian rug on the floor.
Hazel sat down on one of the chairs. Almost at once she
jumped up again. The Yak had appeared.

'Hello,' said Hazel.

The Yak didn't say anything.

'Have you got time to talk?'

'That depends on what you want to talk about,' said
the Yak.

Hazel frowned. Why? Either you have time or you
don't.

'Of course he has time,' said the Yak's mother,
suddenly appearing behind him, and she pushed him
into a room at the other end of the hallway. When she

had finished pushing the Yak she pushed Hazel as well.

It was a big room with large windows and lots of light, and it was full of furniture as well: sofas and armchairs and coffee tables. The Yak was already sitting down. Hazel sat down opposite him. It was the biggest armchair she had ever seen and she sank a long way in. She could see that the Yak had sunk as well.

'Talk!' said the Yak's mother, and she walked out.

Hazel grinned. The Yak watched her suspiciously.

'Did I disturb you?' said Hazel.

'Yes,' said the Yak.

'Oh. What were you doing?'

The Yak didn't answer.

'Is it a secret?' asked Hazel, opening her eyes wide.

The Yak didn't answer that either.

'All right,' said Hazel, 'you don't have to tell me. I didn't mean to disturb you. I just wanted to ask about what you said the other day.'

'About your tower?' said the Yak.

Hazel nodded.

'It will fall,' said the Yak, and he smiled, as if the very thought of such a tower were a joke.

'Why?'

'Why? Because it will, Hazel Green. The first puff of wind will blow it over. And if there is someone sitting on the top, it will blow *him* over as well.'

How could he know that? He only had one glance

at the design. Other people had looked at it for much longer. How could *he* be so sure?

Suddenly the Yak jumped up and ran out of the room. Hazel wondered whether the conversation was over. But a minute later he was back. He had a pen and paper. He perched himself on the armchair next to her and slapped the paper on the coffee table in front of them. Then his hand was whirring over the page, sketching the design.

'5.4 metres high, wasn't it? 2. 3 metres long?' The pen marked the numbers on the page. '1.2 metres wide?'

Hazel nodded, wondering how he could remember the numbers so exactly.

Now the design was in front of her, not like Mandy Furstow's picture, just the bare outline, but accurate.

Still the Yak's hand raced over the page. He was left-handed and the pen whirred across the paper. It drew lines, arrows, angles. *These* had not appeared on Mandy's picture. Now he was writing formulae. Long trails of letters and numbers ran across the page, crossing and recrossing the Moodey Building. Strange words appeared, *sin*, *cos* and *tan*. Now and again the numbers 5.4, 2.3 and 1.2 surfaced. The Yak's pen ran on. Finally it stopped.

There was one last equals sign, and beyond it, in the bottom corner, a number. The Yak underlined it.

He sat back and sank into his chair. 'Even less than I thought.'

Hazel looked at the number. '4.8?'

The Yak nodded. '4.8 kilometres per hour. That's how hard the wind has to blow . . .'

For what?

'. . . to knock your tower over.'

'How hard is that?'

The Yak blew out a gentle puff of air.

Hazel looked back at the page. It was a mess, arrows, lines, pictures, numbers, all running across each other. No, what did the Yak know? Numbers on a page what did it prove? Nothing! She almost laughed. Nothing at all! But she couldn't quite convince herself. In the bottom corner of the page, all by itself and underlined, *that* number stared back at her.

'Are you sure?' said Hazel.

The Yak didn't even answer.

'But what about the real building? The design is exactly modelled on that. We're sitting in it now, and *it* doesn't blow over!'

'No, but it's quite a bit more solid than your crate board tower.'

'But the winds get quite a lot stronger than . . .' Hazel glanced back at the page '. . . *4.8* kilometres.'

'True,' said the Yak, who even seemed to be enjoying himself.

'Well?'

'Well, there's something else you should know about

this building. It has foundations.'

'I know that!'

'Your tower doesn't.'

No, that was a good point. The tower didn't. The tower was going to sit on top of the barrow without a single foundation beneath it.

'But we're going to stick it on. Or maybe even screw it on.'

'Excellent,' said the Yak, 'then the *barrow* will tip as well! The wheels will just make it easier for the whole thing to roll over.' The Yak picked up the page and held it out to Hazel. 'Here, you can check the calculations if you like.'

Hazel took the page reluctantly. She wouldn't know where to begin.

The Yak stood up. 'I think I'll go back to my room now.'

'*No!*' cried Hazel. 'Can't you tell me what's wrong with the tower?'

The Yak rubbed his pointy chin. 'I could . . .' he said.

All at once Hazel knew what he was thinking. 'I'm sorry, I'm sorry!' she cried.

'About what?'

'Your name, you know, the Yak. I didn't mean anything, it just . . .'

She stopped just in time. The Yak was staring at her with bemusement. He didn't know either, obviously.

'Go on,' he said.

'Oh, I'm just sorry other people call you that.'

The Yak shrugged. 'So am I,' he said.

Hazel looked away. The guilt was rising in her. She fought it down. Finally she looked back at the Yak. 'Can't you tell me what's wrong with the tower?'

'It's too high,' said the Yak.

'How high should it be?'

The Yak shrugged.

'Can't you work it out?' said Hazel.

The Yak shrugged again.

'Oh, go on,' said Hazel. 'Please. You know so much maths. What's the point of it if you can't put it to good use?'

The Yak's eyes went wide. 'You call *this* a good use for

mathematics?' he demanded angrily. 'This? A pretend tower?'

'Well, maybe it's not the greatest—'

'This? Do you think a mathematician's mind would concern itself with this? Do you think there would be any great mathematics in the world if *this* was all we thought about?'

We? Who was we?

'Is that what you think?'

'No,' said Hazel quickly.

The Yak was breathing heavily. His chest was heaving.

Hazel spoke very softly. 'What *do* you think about?'

The Yak didn't answer. He sat down again and grabbed the paper out of Hazel's hand. He flipped it over and began scribbling on the back. Soon the page was covered in formulae and calculations again. He finished with a single number, stabbed a line under it, and thrust the page back into Hazel's hand.

'3.7 metres,' he said. 'Not a centimetre higher.'

'The tower? But that'll ruin the proportions!'

The Yak shrugged. He stood up to leave the room. '3.7 metres. That's the limit. I'm telling you. Now you can do what you like.'

9

Behind the Coughlins' fruit shop there were three big storerooms. Two were always full of fruit and vegetables, but the third was never used unless an extra big delivery of potatoes arrived, and that only happened once or twice a year at the most. Otherwise, no one went in there and no one bothered with it. The plaster on its walls was crumbling away. It had a curved ceiling like the inside of a barrel and not a single window. A solitary bare bulb hung from the middle of the roof. When Mr Coughlin switched it on, once or twice a year, it sent a weak yellow light into the corners.

But now, something was happening in the Coughlins' third storeroom: the Moodey Building tower was taking shape. Lying on its side, each day it extended further along the floor like a thick wooden snake.

The Coughlins got used to seeing the children troop in after school, march through the shop and disappear towards the storeroom at the back. A few apples always disappeared along the way as well! Now and again Mr Coughlin would go to have a look at the work and give them another fruit crate to use. The crates came in different sizes and it could be quite a puzzle to work out how to fit them together. The mushroom crates were the hardest to use—they were long and flat and never seemed to fit with anything else. Mandy Furstow and Cobbler were the ones who always seemed to work it out. Mandy drew sketches showing the crates slotting in next to each other—one here, two there, or she would cross it out and start again—while Cobbler stood scratching his fuzzy head and glancing from Mandy's sketch to the tower and back again. Cobbler might whisper an idea in her ear and between them they came up with a solution. Then the others would grab the crates and arrange them as Mandy said, and Sophie Wigg would hammer them together.

Sophie's father owned a hardware shop. He had brought back special nails to use for crates, short, thick and sharp but with a head as wide as a tack, and he had shown her just how much strength to use to knock them in without splitting the wood. Sophie did all the hammering except for the time that Robert Fischer grabbed the hammer and told her it was a job for boys. Well, it wasn't for all boys, apparently. Robert Fischer swung so high and hit the nail so hard that the whole side of the crate split from one end to the other. Not even Leon Davis would let

him touch the hammer again after that,
and Sophie patiently tapped the
nails into the crates, just as her
father had shown her.

Two metres . . . three metres . . .
the tower that would become
the Moodey Building stretched more than *four* metres
across the floor by the time Hazel had finally made up
her mind to speak to the Yak and then came down to
the storeroom to give them the news.

Everyone was there when she arrived. Mandy and
Cobbler were pondering the jigsaw of the latest set of
crates that Mr Coughlin had given them. Leon Davis
was peering over their shoulders, waiting for them to
come up with an answer. Sophie Wigg was sitting down
with her back against the wall, balancing her hammer
on her knees. Paul Boone was munching a pear. The
others were waiting amongst the fruit crates. Marcus

Bunn was playing draughts with Alli Reddick. As soon as Marcus looked up at Hazel, Alli jumped a draught over two of his pieces. Marcus frowned. He was sure those pieces had been safe the last time he looked!

Hazel stopped in the doorway. She glanced at the paper in her hand. 3.7 metres, the Yak had written—the tower already looked too long.

'Hazel Green!' shouted Robert Fischer.

'What?'

'Nothing!' he shouted, and he laughed like a mad hen.

Hazel ignored him. Mandy had just crossed out her latest sketch and was beginning a new one. Hazel told her she could stop.

'Why?' said Cobbler. 'Do you know how to fit them together?'

Hazel shook her head. She sat down on one of the crates. 'How long is the tower now?' she asked.

'3.8 metres,' said Robert Fisher.

'4.1,' said Leon Davis.

'4.2, actually,' said Sophie Wigg, who had checked it just before with a tape measure.

'It's going to be too high,' said Hazel.

'But we haven't even finished,' said Leon Davis.

'It's *already* too high.'

There was silence. Everyone stared at Hazel Green. Only Alli Reddick glanced away for a second and moved something very quickly with her hand.

'Hazel,' said Mandy, 'it's 4.2 metres. And we were going to make it 5.4 metres. Remember? It's not too high. It's still got another 1.2 metres to go.'

Hazel shook her head. 'No. It's already gone too far.'

'Who says?' demanded Leon Davis.

'Yeahhh. *Who says?*' cried Robert  Fischer, jumping up onto a fruit crate and spreading his arms like a bat, as if he were about to launch himself at the person who said 'me'.

'Me,' said Hazel.

Robert's eyes narrowed. He nodded. 'Just checking,' he said, and his arms dropped.

But Leon Davis wasn't so easily satisfied. 'Why?'

'Because it will fall,' said Hazel. 'The slightest puff of wind will blow it over. And the barrow will just make it tip over more easily.'

'There's nothing wrong with the barrow!' said Cobbler.

'Of course there's nothing wrong with the barrow. It's the tower that's the problem. 5.4 metres is just too high. 3.7 is the maximum height.'

'3.7?' said Leon Davis. '*3.7?* Not 3.2, or 2.9?' He looked around the room, appealing to everybody else. 'Hazel seems very sure, doesn't she? But what does she know about building towers? 5.4 was good enough for her yesterday. Now it's 3.7. Tomorrow it might be 1.5.

Who knows how low it will go? Maybe we'll end up using a matchbox instead.'

Everybody laughed, even Mandy Furstow. Only Marcus Bunn bit his lip. His eyes flashed behind his spectacles.

'I believe Hazel,' he cried.

'You would,' said Leon Davis, and Robert Fischer ran over and poked his tongue out in Marcus Bunn's face, waving his arms around and upsetting the draughts board. Alli Reddick started to hit him as the pieces rolled across the floor.

'Well?' said Leon Davis.

'I can prove it,' said Hazel.

She stood up on a fruit crate and took out the piece of paper that the Yak had given her. She held it up with both hands. Leon Davis frowned. He came closer to look at the page.

'What is it?' said Leon.

'Look! See what it says in the bottom corner?'

Everyone gathered around and stared at the paper. No one understood the jottings that covered the page. In the bottom corner the number 3.7 stood out, underlined. But anybody could just write 3.7 and underline it, and then fill the rest of the page with gobbledygook to make it look impressive.

'Did you write this, Hazel?' asked Mandy Furstow.

Hazel hesitated.

'You didn't, did you?' demanded Leon Davis, as if it were some kind of crime to hold up a piece of paper written by someone else.

'She didn't, she didn't!' cried Robert Fischer, leaping from crate to crate like an orang-utan.

'No,' said Hazel. 'The Yak did.'

'The Yak?' At least ten voices cried out together.

Hazel nodded.

'When?'

'Before.'

'Why?'

'He said the building would fall, so I went to see him.'

'You went to see him?'

'The Yak?'

'Hazel went to the Ya-ak! Hazel went to the Ya-ak!'

'Yes!' Hazel shouted, trying to make herself heard over all the voices. 'I went to see the Yak!'

There was silence. Everyone was staring at her again.

'And what did he say?' whispered Mandy Furstow eventually.

'I told you. 3.7 metres is the maximum height. He proved it. Not a centimetre higher.'

'Not a centimetre higher,' said Leon Davis, imitating her in a silly voice.

'I think he's right. He's very clever.'

'He's very clever.' Leon grabbed the paper out of Hazel's hand. 'How do you know he's very clever? This could be anything. I bet you can't even understand it. Go on, tell us what it means.'

Leon held the page up in front of Hazel's nose. Hazel

shook her head. 'Just because
I can't understand it—'

'What does the Yak
know? What does he
know?' repeated Leon
Davis, looking around
at the others. 'Does
he know about building
things? Does he know about
marching? Does he know about . . .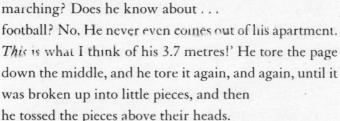
football? No. He never even comes out of his apartment.
This is what I think of his 3.7 metres!' He tore the page
down the middle, and he tore it again, and again, until it
was broken up into little pieces, and then
he tossed the pieces above their heads.

The bits of paper fluttered in
the air and fell on the ground
around them. One of them
settled in Robert Fischer's
hair, and he shook himself
like a jellyfish until it fell off.

'That doesn't change
anything,' said Hazel quietly. 'It
doesn't prove the Yak was wrong.'

'It doesn't prove he was right either. Who thinks the
Yak was right?' Leon looked around the room. 'Well,
who?'

'He *might* be right,' murmured Mandy.

No one else said anything. They didn't want the Yak to be right. They all wanted the building to be as tall as it could be, to rise over everything else in the parade.

'I do . . . I mean, he might be,' said Marcus Bunn eventually.

'You would,' said Leon Davis. He turned back to Hazel. 'You better not say anything to Mr Winkel about this.'

'Of course not,' said Hazel. She had no intention of telling Mr Winkel anything. Mr Winkel was only looking for an excuse to keep them out of the parade. Anything would do.

'Because,' said Leon, as if he were being very clever, 'if you're not careful, Hazel Green, I might just tell Mr Winkel about it myself. I might just tell him you want to change the design. He won't be happy with *that*. And he doesn't like you at all, Hazel Green. He thinks you're rude. He told me himself.'

'Did he?'

'Yes. Mr Winkel and I are quite friendly now. Perhaps I'll just say you're trying to make changes, even though everything's been agreed. Let's see what happens then. Mr Winkel dislikes you so much he might keep you out of the march altogether!'

Robert Fischer laughed, holding his sides. The others were silent, watching to see what would happen. Hazel

Green gazed at Leon. She could read the challenge in his eyes more clearly than if he had spoken it out loud.

She turned and walked out of the storeroom.

Marcus Bunn ran after her. They walked straight past Mr and Mrs Coughlin.

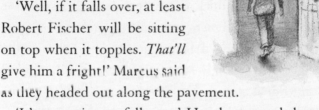

'Well, if it falls over, at least Robert Fischer will be sitting on top when it topples. *That'll* give him a fright!' Marcus said as they headed out along the pavement.

'It's not going to fall over,' Hazel muttered through her teeth.

'No?'

'No. I'm not going to let it.'

They turned the corner. Hazel was setting a fast pace and Marcus was almost running to keep up. Suddenly he stopped. Hazel turned around.

'What is it?'

Marcus was frowning. 'I didn't know you liked the Yak.'

10

'Well, if you ask me,' said Mrs Gluck, 'there's only one thing to do: get Yakov to explain to them.'

Hazel laughed. She picked up a yellow lily that Mrs Gluck needed and handed it to her.

'No?' said Mrs Gluck, carefully sliding the stem of the lily into the arrangement that she was making.

Mrs Gluck stopped for a moment and turned the arrangement around, examining it critically. Hazel examined it as well.

'What do you think, Hazel? Another tulip? It's for a birthday. For a lady who writes books about tapestries.'

'Maybe one more,' said Hazel.

'Yes. Just what I was thinking. A red one.'

Hazel went and picked out a red tulip. Mrs Gluck added it to the arrangement. Now it was complete. But Mrs Gluck didn't turn immediately to her order book. She faced Hazel.

'No?' she said again. 'Why not?'

'I don't think Yakov would do it. Mathematicians have more important things to think about than pretend towers.'

'Is that what he said?'

Hazel nodded.

'But he did the calculations for you, didn't he?'

'Yes, but he didn't seem very happy about it. He seemed angry.'

'Angry? Well, that's very strange.'

Now Mrs Gluck checked her order book. She got up and began collecting flowers from around the workroom. The next arrangement was a display for the hundredth anniversary celebrations of the woodworkers' association. It was going to sit on the top table at their banquet. Soon Mrs Gluck's arms were full of flowers. She had started to hum a tune. She laid the flowers out on the table and went back for more. Hazel began to think she had forgotten all about the Yak and the tower that was too tall.

'You know, it's very easy to misjudge people, Hazel,' said Mrs Gluck suddenly. She was leaning over a bucket full of carnations, looking for those with a tinge of rust in their yellow leaves. 'Especially people you don't know very well. You hardly know Yakov at all.'

'It's not my fault. He never talks to anyone!'

'It doesn't matter whose fault it is. The point is, you might easily misjudge him. If I were you, I would talk to him again to see if he'll explain to the others. I don't really see what you have to lose.'

Hazel wanted to tell her what she had to lose, but she couldn't think of an answer. What *did* she have to lose? The Yak was already angry about having to do the calculations for the tower—at worst, he would get a bit angrier. What difference would it make if he did?

Mrs Gluck began work on the arrangement. Once she had said what she thought about something, she never harped on it. That was one of the best things about her. It was Hazel who must talk to Yakov and therefore it was Hazel who must decide.

Mrs Gluck concentrated on her work, inserting stems into a huge chunk of foam. The woodworkers had asked for an enormous display, something that no one would forget until their next hundredth anniversary. It would take more than two hours to prepare. There must have been forty or fifty flowers already laid out on the table, and Mrs Gluck would add even more later. In her mind she could visualise exactly how she would bring them together, flower by flower, and exactly why, and she would have described it all to Hazel, if she had not seen that Hazel was still deep in thought.

Maybe the Yak wouldn't get angry this time, Hazel was thinking, not if she tried to be especially nice to him. Maybe she should bring him something. Flowers? No. Cakes? Yes, even *mathematicians* must like cakes. Something from one of the bakers. Not from Mr Murray, who had been so nasty when they had that strange talk in his bakery. No, something from Mr Volio. Mr Volio was always happy to see her.

'Samples?' said Mr Volio, 'just a couple of *samples?*'

Hazel nodded, wondering what Mr Volio was getting so worked up about. He always gave her samples. But as soon as he had heard Hazel's voice he had come charging out of the bakery like a big floury bear, and now he stood in front of her, hands on his hips, eyes bulging out of their sockets, saying 'Samples? Just a couple of *samples?*'

Elizabeth, the lady behind the counter, was just as confused as Hazel.

'What would you like?' asked Mr Volio. His tone was harsh and biting. Hazel had never heard him speak like that before.

'Well, anything you think would be nice.'

'Anything I think would be nice? Well, we could give you some strudel, or lemon tarts, or custard fingers.'

'That would be nice.'

'No,' said Mr Volio, putting his forefinger to his lips as if the thought had just occurred to him, 'I know what: we could give you a couple of *Chocolate Dippers* . . .'

'But I thought you weren't going to sell them until—'

'Well, that doesn't matter *now*, does it?'

'All right,' said Hazel, wondering why it didn't matter now, 'if you have a couple . . .'

'And then you could *show* them to Mr Murray instead of just telling him about them!'

Hazel's jaw dropped. Tell Mr Murray about them?

Mr Volio's eyes looked as if they might jump right out at her.

Elizabeth was staring as well. A customer walked in but nobody noticed.

Hazel shook her head.

Mr Volio continued to glare at her.

'No, Mr Volio . . .'

'No, Hazel?'

'No, Mr Volio!'

Now it was Mr Volio who shook his head. His expression softened. But it was not the old, happy Mr Volio, it was a new, sad Mr Volio, sad and disappointed.

'I trusted you, Hazel. We all did. And what did you do? You went and told Mr Murray our most important secret. What did he offer you? A tray of Banbury Buns? A whole Banoffee Pie?'

'He just offered me an éclair . . .' murmured Hazel.

'An éclair! Is that all? Was that the price?'

'No!' cried Hazel. 'I didn't tell him anything.'

'But you took the éclair . . .'

'No, I took a custard tart!'

'So, a custard tart! And don't you know that I would always have given you a custard tart, or anything else for that matter? All you had to do was ask.'

'No, Mr Volio, no!'

'Yes, Hazel, yes. All you had to do was ask. But you didn't, you went to Mr Murray instead. And that was how you repaid our trust.'

'Mr Volio, you don't understand,' cried Hazel.

'I think I do. This is what I understand: Mr Murray knows all about Chocolate Dippers. In fact, he started selling them today! Everyone *loves* them, apparently.'

Hazel stared at Mr Volio in amazement. *Mr Murray selling Chocolate Dippers?* She didn't understand. 'But . . . well, they couldn't be as good as yours, Mr Volio,' she murmured, hoping that would make Mr Volio feel better.

But Mr Volio shook his head, unable to say another word.

'Mr Volio, I didn't tell him. I didn't tell him anything.'

Mr Volio wasn't listening. He was already walking towards the back of the shop, taking slow, weary paces. 'Give her whatever she wants,' he said over his shoulder to Elizabeth, 'if she still has the cheek to ask.'

Hazel didn't ask. She looked away quickly when Elizabeth met her eye.

She left. Outside, all the shops looked bright and welcoming. In Mr Petrusca's shop, the fish gleamed on their bed of crushed, glistening ice. The fishmonger himself was leaning over one of the tanks, snaring a lobster for a customer in a long blue coat. Hazel watched.

The lobster came out, claws thrashing.

What was wrong with Mr Volio? Mr Murray was to blame. *He* was the one Mr Volio should be shouting at. Surely Mr Volio didn't believe that she had given away his secret recipe. Maybe once he had calmed down she could go back and explain.

Hazel sighed. Now for the Yak!

The Yak laughed. He raised his pointy face and laughed at the ceiling.

They were sitting in the same big room in the Yak's apartment. His mother had pushed them in there again. This time her silk gown was a deep plum colour, and her fingernails were plum-coloured as well. Her shoes were yolk yellow. Her hair was auburn and the brooch that she was clutching was gold.

'Tell them?' said the Yak eventually. 'Why should I *tell* them? Did you lose the piece of paper I gave you?'

'No.'

'Well, there's nothing I could tell them that isn't written there.'

'They tore it up.'

'So I suppose they'd punch me in the mouth.'

That was quite clever, thought Hazel, and she would have laughed, but she stopped herself. She didn't think the Yak would appreciate it.

'I was going to bring you a cake,' she said.

The Yak looked at her with curiosity. 'So? What difference would that have made?'

Hazel shrugged. Probably no difference, she thought. 'Why won't you tell them?' she asked, suddenly remembering all the horrible things that Mr Volio had said to her and feeling very sorry for herself.

'Because I can't tell them anything that wasn't written on that page. If they didn't like that page, they're not going to like anything I say to them. That page was the proof, the *mathematical* proof.'

'But they don't *understand* it,' cried Hazel. 'I didn't understand it.'

The Yak shrugged.

'Can't you show them or something?'

'Mathematicians don't *show* . . .'

'Well, what *do* mathematicians do?' demanded Hazel, jumping to her feet.

'Mathematicians think.'

'Really? Is that what they do?'

The Yak nodded smugly, looking up at Hazel out of his chair.

Hazel was breathing heavily. She really wished she had brought some cakes now. She would have shoved them right into the Yak's face.

'Well think about *this*, Mr Mathematician! When they take that tower into the parade, there's going to be a boy sitting on top. And when it falls, he's going to fall as well.

And not only that, when it falls, it's going to fall *on* people. Now, what do you think about *that*?'

'You may well be right,' said the Yak, without showing the least sign of concern.

'So?'

'So, do you think this is news for me? *I* was the one who proved the tower would fall. *I* was the one who calculated how tall it should be. I've done what I had to do.'

Hazel stood for a moment longer. *I've done what I had to do?* What was he talking about? Who decided on the jobs, anyway?

'Well, if that's what being a mathematician means,' she said, 'I'm glad I'm not one!'

Hazel stormed out of the Yak's apartment. She marched wildly to the elevator. She got in when the doors opened and didn't even notice whether it was going up or down. Everything was boiling inside her. The lift stopped on the ground floor. She stormed through the lobby towards the street.

This whole Frogg March idea was becoming a Frogg Nightmare! First Mr Volio and now the Yak! What else could go wrong?

11

There was something strange.

Hazel stopped. She was on the sidewalk. She was still seething. But there was definitely something odd. It was just a feeling. What was it?

For a second Hazel couldn't work it out. Then she realised. Further up the street, someone was pointing at her!

Hazel stared. No, it couldn't be. It looked like Mr Winkel. Now he started hurrying towards her. It *was* Mr Winkel! And not only that, Leon Davis was with him, and so was Sophie Wigg and Robert Fischer and Mandy Furstow, and Mr McCulloch. As they came towards her, other people began to follow, coming out of their shops or turning on the pavement. The Coughlins appeared, and Mr Murray, and Mrs Lundy. It was becoming a crowd. Mr Winkel, who normally never came out of his shop, had actually broken into a run!

Hazel Green turned and began to move away.

'There she is!'

'Stop, Hazel Green!'

Hazel began to run. She raced into the Moodey Building. The shouts grew behind her. All the elevators were on the upper floors. She ran out into the courtyard and set off for the rusty fire escape door on the other side.

'*Hazel Green!*'

She ran.

'*Hazel Green! Stop!*'

The door was closed. She couldn't open it from the outside. Hazel turned, her back to the wall. Leon Davis was closest, halfway across the courtyard. Mr Winkel was running to keep up. Others were pouring out of the lobby behind him.

'Why are you running?' cried Mr Winkel, gasping for breath.

Why was *she* running? Hazel watched him suspiciously. He came closer. Soon the others arrived. There was a crowd of twenty or thirty people approaching her. Most of them had just joined in the rush and didn't even know what it was about. Mr Petrusca was holding a fish by the gills, and Mr Antoniou, the tailor, had a dozen pins pressed between his lips. Half the customers in the *Vienna* café had jumped up from their tables to see what was happening.

'So, Hazel,' said Mr Winkel when he had recovered his breath, 'you want to interfere some more with the parade?'

Hazel glared at Leon Davis.

'I knew you meant trouble, from the very moment you stepped foot in my shop. Children have no place in parades. I said it then and I should have listened to what I said.'

'What about Leon?' said Hazel.

'He's not a troublemaker like you,' retorted Mr Winkel, and he put a hand on Leon's shoulder.

Leon smiled angelically. Hazel was almost sick. She glanced around at all the faces opposite her. Hardly anyone met her eyes. Even Mr McCulloch's gaze shifted quickly when she looked at him.

'Now, you listen to me, Hazel Green. I know you're interfering and trying to change everything. Leon told me all about it. Well, you leave the display to Leon. From now on, he's in charge. Any more interference, and you won't even march!'

Leon smiled his disgusting smile again.

'Understand?'

'No!' It was Mr Volio, who had just arrived. Every face turned towards him. There was a deathly silence: everyone wondered what he was going to say next.

Mr Volio didn't look as if he'd calmed down. In fact, he looked even angrier than before.

'Hazel Green shouldn't march at all. If she marches, Arthur, *I* don't.'

'Why?' said Mr Winkel, in a tone of voice that

sounded as if he didn't care why at all.

'Hazel knows,' said Mr Volio, fixing Hazel with a dark gaze.

'What about Mr Murray?' cried Hazel, '*he's* the one who stole your Chocolate Dippers!'

Mr Murray laughed. 'Stole? Me? *Invented*, you mean!' He looked meaningfully at Mr Volio. 'You'd better have proof if you say otherwise, Stephen Volio.'

Mr Volio bit his lip. Then he pointed at Hazel. His finger shook with rage. 'If *she* marches, I don't.'

'But you *always* march,' said Mr Winkel. 'Who'll carry the banner?'

'It's me or her,' said Mr Volio.

Mr Winkel shrugged his shoulders, sighing, but he couldn't keep the satisfaction off his face. 'Well, Hazel, I'm afraid you've gone too far. It looks like there's no march for you.'

'We'll see about that,' muttered Hazel to herself.

'We certainly will,' said Mr Winkel. He looked around at the others. They looked back at him. No one knew what to do next.

'Mr Winkel,' said Leon Davis, 'don't worry about her. Why don't you come and see how much of the tower we've done already? It's almost ready for painting.'

'Yes,' said Mr Winkel. 'That sounds like a very good idea.' He put his hand on Leon's shoulder. Leon threw one last smirk at Hazel as they walked away.

Mr Volio glared for a moment longer at Hazel as well. Then he left. Mr Petrusca glanced down at the fish in his hand, as if only now he realised that he was holding it, and turned. One by one, all the others departed. The customers from the *Vienna* café went back to see if their coffees had got cold.

Only Hazel remained. She sat down against the wall. Anyone else would have burst into tears, but not Hazel Green.

 She looked up at the building, as she had looked up on that day when she first had the idea to build a replica of it for the parade. On all four sides, rows of windows reached high above her, climbing into the sky. They gazed down like dark, unblinking eyes, as if waiting to see what she would do.

'So,' she said to herself, 'they don't want me to march. Well, we'll just have to change their minds!'

But how she was going to do it, she couldn't quite say.

Above her, in one of the windows, there was a movement. Hazel didn't see it. It was the Yak, who had watched everything that happened.

12

At six o'clock, Hazel came out onto her balcony. The air was still chilly from the night, and the tiles were cool with dew. Somewhere, a bird twittered. Mr Volio appeared on the pavement. He stretched out his arms and threw back his head to warm his face in the sunlight. When he opened his eyes he spotted Hazel looking down at him. He went back into his bakery.

It had become very strange, going to school each morning. Everyone else walked in groups, talking excitedly about the preparations for the Frogg March. Robert Fischer flitted from one bunch to another like a herring. But whenever Hazel approached, everyone somehow melted away, falling behind or rushing ahead until she was by herself again. Leon Davis smirked. Sometimes Mandy Furstow or Hamish Rae walked with her for a while, but the lure of the others always drew them away eventually. Even Marcus Bunn skipped off to add his opinions to the conversations about the Frogg March. After all, *he* was going to march, and Hazel wasn't.

Under the light of the bare bulb in the Coughlin's third storeroom, the tower continued to grow. Soon it had reached its full height of 5.4 metres. It was still lying on its side and no one had tried to raise it. Now the painting had begun. The ground floor was already finished, and each shop was shown individually just as it appeared if you walked around the building.

Hazel knew what was happening. Each day she overheard the others talking about the tower's progress. But for the first time in her life she was not involved. She walked by herself. It was strange and she didn't enjoy it. Like the Yak, she found herself on the outside, looking on.

He was waiting for her, one day, after school, at the entrance to the Moodey Building. As usual, he had walked back by himself and arrived before anyone else. The others glanced at him with curiosity. Marcus Bunn walked past with his nose in the air, pretending not to notice. He'll walk straight into something, thought Hazel, if he isn't careful.

'Where can we talk?' said the Yak.

Hazel frowned. 'What do you have to say?'

'Not here!'

'All right,' said Hazel, shrugging, 'Rubbish Alley.'

Hazel led the way to the lane at the back. The Yak looked around at the rubbish containers and the dark, damp walls. He wrinkled up his nose at the dank smell.

Hazel watched him. 'I don't suppose *mathematicians* are used to places like this.'

The Yak didn't reply.

'You've never been here before, have you?' said Hazel.

The Yak shook his head.

'Well, it's not the prettiest place, but it's quiet . . . apart from the rats!'

Hazel laughed as the Yak looked around anxiously.

'They don't usually come out in the day, but we can come back at night to see them, if you like.'

'No,' said the Yak, 'it's all right.'

Suit yourself, thought Hazel. The rats won't miss *you*, either.

Hazel waited. The Yak was taking an awfully long time to speak. Maybe he had decided that he didn't want to say anything, after all.

'Why did the fat man say you couldn't march?' he blurted out suddenly.

'Which fat man?' said Hazel.

'The man in the courtyard when all those people were there.'

'Oh, that's who you're talking about. Mr Volio.'

'Is that his name?'

'He's one of the bakers.'

'Well, why did he say it?'

'He thinks I told a secret. He thinks I gave away his new recipe.'

'His new recipe?' The Yak's eyes narrowed. 'And did you?'

'Everyone thinks I did.'

'But *did* you?'

'What do you think?'

The Yak didn't answer. He screwed his pointy face up tight, as if he had a pea lodged painfully inside his nose. It was a funny expression and Hazel almost laughed out loud.

'I didn't,' said Hazel.

'I didn't think so,' said the Yak, relaxing his face.

'Why not?'

The Yak didn't answer the question. 'I saw it, you know. From my room. When the fat man said you couldn't march.'

'He isn't *fat*,' said Hazel, who still couldn't help liking Mr Volio, even after everything that had happened.

'Well, I saw it, even if he isn't fat. But he looks fat, Hazel Green.'

'Maybe he's a little bit fat.'

The Yak smiled. Hazel laughed. 'He bakes pastries all day,' she said, 'and he needs to taste them. Obviously he's going to be a little bit fat!'

The Yak nodded. 'Obviously.'

The Yak was silent again. Hazel began to look around the alley for a rat that she could show him. She was sure he'd be interested in seeing one.

'It isn't fair,' said the Yak.

Hazel shrugged. Why did he care? 'I didn't think mathematicians would worry about things like that.'

The Yak bit his lip. He made his screwed-up face again. This time Hazel did laugh. The Yak blushed in embarrassment.

'I'm sorry,' said Hazel. 'Your face looked funny, that's all.'

Now the Yak blushed even harder. He almost ran away.

'Don't go!' cried Hazel.

The Yak looked at her hesitantly.

'Why did you want to tell me that you saw it?' asked Hazel.

'Because I didn't think you could have done it— whatever it was that made the fat man say you shouldn't march. And I knew you weren't *interfering*, because it was my calculation, and all you were doing was trying to make sure they built the tower properly.'

'Well, you're right about one thing,' said Hazel. 'It isn't fair.'

'Then you should do something about it.'

'I know I should do something about it. Why? Do you want to help me?'

The Yak frowned. He didn't look very certain.

'Well?'

The Yak nodded.

'Swear on your nose!'

'Swear on *what*?'

'On your nose.' Hazel stared at him in amazement.

How could a boy live in the Moodey Building for a whole year and not know what it was to swear on your nose? Hazel explained what it meant. The Yak said it was ridiculous. It *was* ridiculous, that was precisely why he had to do it. The Yak thought that was even more ridiculous. Hazel agreed but there was nothing she could do about it. Finally the Yak put a finger on his nose and rapidly mumbled a few words.

'Good,' said Hazel, 'now, what do you think we should do?'

'I'm not sure,' said the Yak.

'Of course,' said the Yak, 'we could just forget about the fat man—'

'Mr Volio,' said Hazel.

'Mr Volio. We could just forget about him. You could go to that other man—'

'Mr Winkel.'

'Mr Winkel. You could go to him and explain that the tower's too high. He'd be so happy you warned him, he'd let you march for sure.'

'No. He wouldn't believe me. He'd think I was just trying to upset everything. He loves Leon Davis so much he believes anything he says.'

'Well . . .' The Yak hesitated. 'I suppose I could go to Mr Winkel and prove that the tower's too high, just like I proved it for you.'

Hazel considered. They were sitting amongst all the sofas and armchairs in the front room of the Yak's apartment. The Yak's mother had shown hardly any surprise when Hazel turned up with her son. This time her gown was turquoise and her shoes were the colour of ivory. Her hair was brown and the brooch in her hand was a shiny, burnished copper.

Hazel tried to imagine the Yak doing his mathematical calculations for Mr Winkel on the counter in the leathergoods shop. No, Mr Winkel wouldn't understand a single line. You would have to be a mathematical expert to follow it. Mr Winkel would throw them both out.

Hazel shook her head. 'That wouldn't work. Mr Volio's the one. The only way is to get Mr Volio on our side. Then *he* can go to Mr Winkel. Mr Winkel will believe him.'

The Yak didn't look convinced.

'I'm telling you, it's the only way.'

The Yak sighed. 'Tell me about Mr Volio again.'

Hazel told him the whole story once more, about the top secret Chocolate Dipper that she had tasted for Mr Volio, and about the way Mr Murray had questioned her, and about the way Mr Volio had accused her of telling the secret.

'But you *didn't* tell the secret,' said the Yak when Hazel had finished.

'Of course not!'

'But Mr Murray found out anyway.'

'Obviously. He's been selling Chocolate Dippers for a week.'

'Then what I don't understand,' said the Yak, frowning with intense concentration, 'is why Mr Murray bothered to ask you at all! He got the information somewhere else anyway.'

'True,' said Hazel. 'I don't understand it either.'

'Why would you ask someone for information you already have?' murmured the Yak, going over it in his mathematical mind. 'It isn't logical. Why? Why would you bother?'

'Exactly. Why would you bother?'

'To make people *think* you got the information from the second person,' said Mrs Gluck, when Hazel repeated the question in her workroom. 'Is that possible?'

'I don't know,' said Hazel, who hadn't thought about that. 'Yes, I suppose it is.'

'Well,' said Mrs Gluck, 'that must be it.'

'Then all we have to work out,' said the Yak, when Hazel came back the next day and told him what Mrs Gluck had said, 'is who else might have given the information.'

'No one,' said Hazel. 'No one else knew.'

'No one else?'

'Well, only the people who work in Mr Volio's bakery.

There's Mr Volio himself, and the two Mrs Volios, and Martin, and Andrew McAndrew, but none of them would tell.'

'Andrew McAndrew?' said the Yak, thinking that was a very suspicious name and might easily belong to a spy.

'*He'd* never tell.'

'Who else, then?'

'No one else. Only . . .' Hazel paused, her eyes went wide.

'Only what?'

'Only . . .'

'*What?*' cried the Yak.

'I've just had an idea.'

13

The bakers' apprentices were a mysterious bunch. They arrived in the night and left in the morning, and worked out of sight in the heat of the bakeries, so no one really knew who they were. Mr Volio had four and Mr Murray had three, and Mr Volio's were as round and plump as Mr Volio himself, from all the pastries they were forced to eat, while Mr Murray's were as thin and lean as Mr Murray, from all the pastries they *weren't* allowed to eat. But whether they worked for one baker or the other, their faces were always covered in flour, their aprons smeared with jam and their hands speckled with dough. And they were always getting into trouble. Who else could it have been, but one of the apprentices, who gave away the secret of the Chocolate Dipper?

But how could they prove it?

'Simple,' said the Yak, who thought there was a mathematical proof for everything. 'By subtraction. If it wasn't Mr Volio, and it wasn't the Mrs Volios, and it wasn't Martin, and it wasn't Andrew McAndrew . . .' the Yak paused, because he still thought that was a suspicious name, whatever Hazel said, '. . . and if it wasn't *you*, and if that's all the people who knew, apart from the apprentices, then, by subtraction, it must be the apprentices who told.'

'But no one else believes it wasn't me,' Hazel pointed out.

'True,' said the Yak, but he wasn't prepared to give up his mathematical proof at the first objection. 'Then the only other thing we have to do is prove it wasn't you.'

'But there isn't any way to do that.'

'Yes,' said the Yak, 'that is a problem.'

'So we have to prove the apprentices did it.'

'Well, we could try to do that, but then we wouldn't be proving it by subtraction.'

'So?'

'Well, proof by subtraction is the most elegant kind of proof. It's my favourite. And besides, we could do it right now, on paper.'

Hazel was sorry they couldn't use the Yak's favourite kind of proof, but that wasn't the most important thing on her mind.

'No, we'll just have to catch them, the apprentices who did it.'

The Yak gazed coolly at Hazel. Catch them? That didn't sound like his kind of proof. For a start, you didn't catch people by sitting at your desk, with pen and paper. People didn't get caught with mathematical symbols and complicated equations.

'I won't be able to do it by myself,' said Hazel.

'Won't you?'

Hazel fixed the Yak with her most penetrating gaze, which she used only in the most extreme circumstances. It almost hurt to gaze like that—she hardly dared imagine what it must be like to be on the receiving end.

'What?' cried the Yak.

'You swore to help.'

'I have helped.'

'On your nose. You swore on your nose!'

'That's ridiculous.'

Hazel continued to gaze. Her eyes were really starting to hurt. 'On your nose,' she repeated ominously .

'Mathematicians don't—'

'Don't tell me what mathematicians don't do. Mathematicians don't watch while other people are being accused of telling secrets in the courtyard, do they?'

'No,' mumbled the Yak.

'No,' said Hazel, although she didn't know why they shouldn't. It was probably quite an interesting thing to watch, after all. 'And they don't go to Rubbish Alley, do they?'

'No.'

'Or swear on their nose.'

The Yak shook his head.

'Well, you should have thought about all of that before. Because mathematicians don't break their promises, do they?'

'No,' said the Yak, 'they don't.'

In fact, Hazel could have used the help of more than just one other person, but she couldn't think of anyone else who would be willing. Marcus Bunn, for instance, had almost stopped talking to her after she had been seen again with the Yak. Sometimes he came up alongside her, and peered through his glasses like a curious owl, as if he couldn't quite believe that this was the same Hazel Green whom he had known before. And if Marcus didn't want to help her, it was hardly likely that anyone else would!

The next morning, just before six o'clock, Hazel slipped out of the apartment building. She crossed the street and walked quickly until she came to a lamp post that stood across the road from Mr Volio's bakery. The door to the bakery was still closed. Inside, she knew, everybody would be sitting around the big kneading table, drinking cocoa. Hazel turned sideways to hide

herself behind the post. She looked at her watch. She
wasn't really sure that the Yak would come. He *said* he
would come, but they had agreed to meet at six, and
there was no sign of him.

Hazel looked at her watch again.

She heard footsteps. Someone was coming towards
her from the direction of the Moodey Building. He was
dressed completely in black, with a black balaclava over
his head. All you could see were his eyes.

'It's me,' said the Yak.

'What are you *wearing*?' she demanded in a whisper.

'Perfect, isn't it?' The Yak's voice was muffled by the
balaclava. 'No one will recognise me in this.'

'No, and no one will notice you either, not with all the
other millions of people walking around with balaclavas
on!' She reached out suddenly and grabbed the balaclava
off the Yak's head.

'Give it back!' cried the Yak, whose hair was all messed up. With his pointy chin, he looked even funnier than usual.

'No. Don't be ridiculous. And keep your voice down.'

'Give it back, I said. Give it back right—'

'Shhhh!' Hazel grabbed the Yak's arm and spun him around. The door to Mr Volio's bakery had just opened.

Looking at the reflection in a shop window, they watched what was happening behind them across the street. A woman came out. It was old Mrs Volio. The door stayed open.

'Just try to look like you're looking in the window,' whispered Hazel.

'I am looking in the window!' hissed the Yak.

'Yes, but try not to look like you're looking at their reflection.'

'How?'

Hazel didn't know how. 'Just try.'

'Are *you* trying?'

'Shhhh!'

'Stop telling me to Shhhh!'

'Shhhh! Look, here they are.'

The four apprentices were coming out of the bakery. Hazel and the Yak watched their reflections. They stood on the pavement for a minute, talking. Then they split up. Three went one way, and the fourth turned in the opposite direction and went off by himself.

'Okay, let's wait a few seconds,' said Hazel. 'I'll take the three who went together. You take the other one.'

'Give me my balaclava.'

'Not if you're going to put it on. Swear on your nose.'

'Forget my nose! Give me the balaclava or I'm not following anybody.'

Hazel sighed. She handed over the balaclava. They split up. Hazel set off after the three apprentices who were walking together. The Yak followed the solitary one. Hazel glanced back over her shoulder. Sure enough, the great superspy of a Yak had stopped and was fitting the balaclava over his head.

Hazel's three apprentices dawdled along the empty pavements. They shouted and laughed, and sometimes stopped to punch each other. They passed a man walking a chihuahua and they all stopped to make fun of the miniature dog. The man hurried away, which made them laugh even more. After a couple of blocks,

one of them said goodbye and disappeared into an apartment building. The other two walked on. They didn't say much to each other, as if it were the first one who kept the conversation going when they were together. After a while they reached a café and that was where they parted. One of them went inside. Hazel followed the other one, who kept walking. He turned a corner and stood at a bus stop. Ten minutes later an early bus came and he got on. Hazel watched the bus pull away. When she went past the café again, she saw the other apprentice sitting by himself at a table in the window, digging into a big plate of fried eggs.

'And what about your one?' said Hazel to the superspy, when they met again after school.

The Yak shrugged. 'He walked to the park and bought a pretzel.'

'A pretzel?'

'Yes. I'm amazed there's someone who sells pretzels so early in the morning.'

Hazel didn't care about pretzel-sellers, it was apprentices who concerned her. 'And?'

'It was a very good pretzel.'

'How do you know?'

'I bought one myself. It was almost a shame to eat it. It was a perfect figure of 8, which of course immediately reminded me of numbers, and then suddenly I remembered a mathematical problem I've been working

on, which has been worrying me for weeks, and . . . and
I think I've solved it!' said the Yak, getting quite excited.
'Maybe it was the fresh morning air, or the pretzel, I'm

not sure, but mathematicians should definitely consider
getting out into the park when they're working on
difficult problems. You see, suddenly it came to me. It
was a complicated problem with sets, but then I realised
that if I replaced the—'

'Yakov,' said Hazel, trying to be patient, 'what
happened to the apprentice?'

'The apprentice? Yes, well, he . . . bought a pretzel, as
I said.'

'And then?'

'Then? Then . . . I solved that problem. I already told
you about that.'

'And the apprentice?'

'Well, to be honest, I'm not too sure about the apprentice after that. You see, the problem was very complicated. *Very* complicated. It took all my attention.'

'So you don't know what happened to the apprentice?'

'Correct. I don't know.'

Hazel stared at the Yak, wondering what you could do with a mathematician.

'I don't suppose you'd like to see the solution to the problem?' said the Yak.

Hazel shook her head. The Yak's problem wasn't the one that interested her. She had a different question: what was going on with this apprentice? Why would he go to the park and buy a pretzel? For a start, he could have got a pretzel in Mr Volio's bakery, and he wouldn't even have had to pay for it. And besides, what was he doing in the park so early in the morning after a whole night's work? Why didn't he have breakfast or go home to bed like the others?

14

The same thing happened the next morning.

Hazel went after the three apprentices, who repeated almost the same pattern as on the morning before, except both of the last two apprentices got on the bus together. Meanwhile, the Yak's apprentice had gone back to the park and bought a pretzel again. Of course, this time the Yak was determined to concentrate, and in fact he was able to report that after the apprentice bought the pretzel he sat down on one of the park benches and started to eat it, and he might even have been able to report what happened after that, except just at that moment it suddenly occurred to him that there might be a second way of solving the problem from the day before, and if it had been anything other than that, of course, he would have had no difficulty concentrating on the apprentice and his pretzel, but *that*, well, how could you stop your mind thinking about that, after all, a *second* solution, no, you just couldn't expect anyone to be able to resist it, although he tried, of course, he tried very hard, but really, it just wasn't possible, and in short—he had no idea what happened after that. No idea at all.

'None?' whispered Hazel.

The Yak shook his head, grinning. 'But I can show you the second solution, if you like. It's much more elegant than the first, and it uses subtraction!'

Excellent, thought Hazel, it uses subtraction. Perhaps she should use a bit of subtraction on the Yak.

The next morning, the apprentices split up just as before. But this time Hazel followed the solitary apprentice. The Yak crept behind her, wearing his balaclava.

The apprentice turned the corner of the Moodey Building. Sure enough, just as the Yak had said, he crossed the street and turned into another street that led to the park. He went in through the entrance where the big iron gates had just been opened. Then he followed a wide gravel path that led to a pond with a fountain. All around it were trees. Beside the pond, just as the Yak had said, was a man selling fresh pretzels. The apprentice bought one.

The apprentice went and sat on a bench near the pond. Hazel veered off into the trees to hide. The Yak, meanwhile, had marched right up to the pretzel-seller! Hazel watched in dismay. The apprentice was watching as well. He probably even recognised the boy in the black balaclava, who was becoming a regular visitor to the park. The Yak picked up *two* pretzels. Hazel watched as he paid for them. The apprentice watched too. If the Yak came over to give her one of the pretzels, the apprentice would see her. He would recognise her. Everything would be ruined!

Hazel ran. She raced through the trees. Her feet crunched over dry leaves and she skipped over fallen branches. She ran in a long arc behind the apprentice's back and she didn't stop until she was on the other side of the pond. She hid behind a tree. The Yak was still standing in the path, holding the pretzels, looking for her. Hazel held her breath. As long as he didn't call out her name! If he did, it was all over. The apprentice would know she was there.

The Yak was still looking. Hazel could see the puzzlement on his pointy face. She hardly dared to breathe.

The Yak opened his mouth. Hazel flinched, waiting to hear the sound, as if his voice were a raised stick that was about to strike her.

'Why don't you sit down?'

It was the apprentice who had called out. He was getting sick of seeing the Yak standing there.

The Yak's shoulders twitched. The apprentice wasn't meant to notice him! In his confusion, he forgot about calling out for Hazel. He sat down on a bench.

The Yak threw the apprentice a cautious glance. He took off his balaclava and nibbled one of the pretzels. The apprentice watched him curiously. The Yak glanced back at him. He chewed his pretzel. The Yak's glances became fewer and fewer. After a while he stopped looking at the apprentice altogether and ended up gazing at something on the ground, maybe a pebble or maybe nothing at all, occasionally nibbling at his pretzel. Hazel watched in disbelief. What difficult and complicated equations were going through his head? She didn't know, and neither did the apprentice, who watched him for a while longer and then lost interest. At that moment Hazel lost interest as well. Someone else had just come into the park.

The new arrival stopped at the pretzel cart. Hazel peered as hard as she could. The figure was somehow familiar, thin and gangly. Hazel was sure she knew him, but he was still too far away. He took a pretzel and began to walk towards the pond. A branch got in the way and Hazel couldn't see him. Then he reappeared, much closer now, shouting something to the apprentice who sat on the bench.

Hazel gasped.

She knew that face. She knew who it was.

It was Sebastian, the fruit-slicing apprentice from Mr Murray's bakery!

Sebastian sat down on the bench next to the apprentice from Mr Volio's bakery. They munched their pretzels, pausing to talk and joke. Hazel couldn't hear what they said. Later they jumped up and raced each other out of the park.

And all the time the Yak sat, gazing at the ground, nibbling on his pretzel, lost in thought.

15

'It's not really *proof*, is it?' said Mrs Gluck.

'I saw them together!' said Hazel. 'They were talking to each other.'

'So? They're allowed to talk to each other, aren't they?'

'Well, there's no proof against *me*, is there? Only Mr Murray who says I told him, and he's lying.'

'True,' said Mrs Gluck. She frowned in thought, gathering up stems and leaves and odd ends of twine from her table. She had finished the last arrangement for

the day, and the bouquets stood all around her in the workroom, ready to be collected. Every one was individual and different from the others. 'What about Yakov?' she said suddenly. 'He was sitting near them. Perhaps he heard something.'

'Not the Yak,' said Hazel dismissively. 'He didn't hear anything. He didn't even *see* anything.'

Mrs Gluck laughed. 'Hazel, that's a terrible name to call him.'

'Everyone calls him that,' said Hazel, not bothering to tell Mrs Gluck exactly *who* it was who had thought of the name.

Mrs Gluck dropped the offcuts into the big garbage pail under the table. 'How do you know he didn't hear anything?'

Hazel laughed. 'The Yak doesn't hear or see, Mrs Gluck. He just *thinks*.'

'Thinks?'

'Mathematically. That's all he does. You could drop a bomb on his head and he wouldn't even notice, not if he was working on a mathematical problem.'

'You should bring him here with you one day. I'd like to meet this boy who thinks all the time.'

'No, he wouldn't come. He'd say "Mathematicians don't look at flowers", or something like that. Whenever he doesn't want to do something it's because mathematicians don't do it. I think he just makes it up. Do you know any mathematicians, Mrs Gluck?'

'I'm not sure.' Mrs Gluck sat down beside the table. She folded her hands together and rubbed her knuckles, which always ached a bit after a whole day spent working with flowers. 'Wait, we do have an engineer. He comes to get flowers for his mother. He's very precise. He always comes on the third Saturday of every month and the second Monday following. I don't think I would have noticed how precise he was if he hadn't explained it to me himself. Except once he came on a Tuesday, and he was so embarrassed he could barely tell us which flowers he wanted. He didn't need to, of course, because we already knew. Lilies, freesias and jonquils if they're in season. But he's an engineer, not a mathematician.'

'Engineers have to be good at maths.'

'I'm sure they do,' said Mrs Gluck. 'There must be *some* mathematicians who like flowers.'

'No, it wouldn't surprise me if there weren't, Mrs Gluck.'

Mrs Gluck frowned. It was very odd, that there might be a whole group of people who didn't like flowers. But she *didn't* know any mathematicians, so maybe it was true. On the other hand, maybe some of her customers were mathematicians and just hadn't told her. Customers didn't always tell you everything you needed to know.

'No,' said Hazel, 'the Yak can't prove the apprentice told the secret any more than I can.'

'And you *can't*.'

'No, but I saw them talking. How else could Mr Murray have found out?'

'I don't know,' said Mrs Gluck, 'but you can't just go up to Mr Volio and say that one of his apprentices told

Mr Murray. You can't prove it, Hazel, and you might get him into trouble.'

Hazel didn't care if the apprentice did get into trouble. He *had* told about the Chocolate Dipper, she was certain. There was no one else who could have done it. Besides, you could almost prove it by subtraction.

Mrs Gluck didn't know anything about proving by subtraction. 'But I do know this,' she said, 'you can only tell what you genuinely saw and heard, Hazel. You tell Mr Volio that, and *he* can decide what it means.'

It wasn't necessarily such a simple thing to go and see Mr Volio. Once it had been the easiest thing in the world. But Mr Volio no longer called Hazel into his bakery to give her chocolate rollos and cups of hot cocoa. In fact, Hazel was fairly sure that she was not particularly welcome in his bakery at all. No one had actually said so, of course, but she just had a feeling.

Yet there was no point in having followed the apprentice and having discovered how Mr Murray found out about the Chocolate Dipper if she wasn't going to tell Mr Volio. That was the whole reason for it, after all!

She went into the bakery late in the afternoon. Elizabeth glanced at her with an odd, frozen expression on her face, as if she wanted to smile at her but knew she wasn't supposed to. Hazel waited while she served a lady. The customer wanted only three little pastries but it took an awfully long time because she couldn't make up her mind. Even after she had managed to select two of the cakes she just couldn't decide about the last. Finally she turned to Hazel and asked her which one *she* would choose.

Hazel surveyed the pastries behind the glass. Eventually she pointed at a raisin slice coated with fig jelly. 'All right, one of those,' said the lady with a sigh of relief, and Elizabeth couldn't hide a grateful smile at Hazel, even though she wasn't supposed to.

'Where's Mr Volio?' said Hazel when the lady had gone.

'He's not here,' said Elizabeth.

'Will he be back soon?'

'Yes.'

'Then I'll wait,' said Hazel. 'You don't mind, do you?'

'*I* don't mind,' said Elizabeth. 'But I don't think Mr Volio will be pleased to see you.'

'Maybe he will,' said Hazel.

Hazel leaned against the wall. She looked at the pastries. Elizabeth began to clean up behind the counter. The minutes passed. Someone came in and bought some bread. Then the shop was empty once more. Still Hazel waited. Elizabeth glanced at her. She swept some crumbs off a shelf and glanced at her again. Finally she turned around and said: 'I can't let you stand there like that. You must be hungry. I know I'm not meant to give you anything, but . . .' She reached down and picked up one of the raisin slices and held it out to Hazel.

Hazel screwed up her nose. 'I don't like *them*.'

'But didn't you just tell that lady to buy one?'

'Yes, but I didn't like her. I don't like people who can't make up their minds. Do you, Elizabeth?'

'No,' said Elizabeth, trying to stifle her laughter. 'Here, I know what you like,' she said, handing over a custard tart.

'That's much better,' said Hazel. 'Thank you.'

'Just don't tell Mr Volio I gave it to you.'

'No, I wouldn't do that,' said Hazel, and she didn't need to, because just as she took her first taste of the custard tart, the door of the bakery swung open and in walked Mr Volio himself, carrying a sack of flour.

The sack hit the floor. Mr Volio stood there open-mouthed and wide-eyed. His nostrils flared above the thick handlebars of his moustache.

'Hello, Mr Volio,' said Hazel.

Mr Volio didn't answer. His face went red. It looked like there were some words boiling in his throat, but they just couldn't find their way out.

'This is a very good tart,' said Hazel, because she couldn't think of anything else to say, and it looked like Mr Volio might explode if he had to keep trying to get the words out. Besides, it *was* a very good tart. Hazel had almost forgotten how good Mr Volio's pastries were.

'Please don't blame Elizabeth for giving it to me,' she added.

Mr Volio gave Elizabeth a quick, sharp glance, but immediately looked back at Hazel.

'Why are you here, Hazel?' he said.

Hazel sighed with relief. At least Mr Volio was talking again! She had been worried that his throat was going to be blocked up forever.

'Well?' said Mr Volio. 'I haven't got any more secrets for you to give away, so you're wasting your time.'

'Maybe I have a secret for you,' said Hazel.

Mr Volio snorted. 'There's no use trying to convince me to let you march. You're welcome to the custard tart and I hope you enjoy it.' Mr Volio bent down to pick up the sack.

'But maybe I really do have a secret you want to hear,' said Hazel.

Mr Volio glanced up at her. 'What secret?'

'About who really did tell Mr Murray about the Chocolate Dipper.'

'I know who told him about the Chocolate Dipper: you!'

'Are you sure?'

'Perfectly.'

'Well, then you won't want to hear what I have to say.'

Mr Volio straightened up. His eyes narrowed. Suddenly he waved a flour-covered finger. 'If you're playing games with me, Hazel Green, I promise you, you'll be in even bigger trouble. Not being able to march on Frogg Day will be the least of your problems!'

'All right,' said Hazel.

Mr Volio gazed at her for a moment longer, then he bent down, picked up the sack, slung it over his shoulder and walked past her towards the back of the shop. At the door to the bakery he stopped and turned around.

'Well,' he said, 'what are you waiting for? If you have something to tell me you'd better come in here.'

Mr Volio paced around the kneading table. His brow was furrowed. His expression was troubled. Now and again he glanced at Hazel, who sat on a stool beside the oven, which was just beginning to warm up. There was no one else in the bakery. Not even the apprentices had arrived.

'You say you saw them together?' asked Mr Volio, even though he had asked the question four times already.

Hazel nodded.

'But you didn't hear anything?'

Hazel shook her head. She had told Mr Volio that four times as well.

'In the park? . . . Eating a pretzel?' Suddenly Mr Volio stopped, with an expression of real pain on his face, as if that were the very worst part of it, that one of his apprentices bought pretzels from somebody else instead of taking them from his own bakery. 'I would have given him pretzels,' he murmured, beginning to pace again, 'as many as he wanted.'

'I don't think the pretzels are that important, Mr Volio,' said Hazel.

Mr Volio shook his head. Hazel didn't know if that meant he agreed or not.

'To be honest, I can't say I heard him tell about the Chocolate Dipper,' said Hazel.

'It was yesterday?'

'Yesterday.'

'Well, Mr Murray found out about the Chocolate Dipper weeks ago.'

'But they must meet there every day. I'm sure they were going there before as well. Mr Volio, what I *can* tell you is that I never said anything about the Chocolate Dipper. Never, Mr Volio. Not to Mr Murray, not to *anybody*.'

Mr Volio stopped on the other side of the table. He gazed at Hazel. Then he nodded his head. 'I know, Hazel.' He buried his face in his hands. When he looked up again, his cheeks were covered in flour. 'Perhaps deep down I always knew you hadn't told. But it was easier to believe it was you than somebody from my own bakery.'

'It's all right, Mr Volio.'

'No, Hazel, it's not all right. I did not believe you, and you had never lied to me before. But those apprentices— oh, they're terrible boys, Hazel. Always telling tales,

pretending they're sick—anything to get out of doing a real day's work.'

'Weren't you the same when you were an apprentice, Mr Volio?'

'Of course I was the same! But that was different. And never, *never* would I have betrayed my master.'

Hazel nodded. For an apprentice to betray his master must be a terrible thing, and since she was not a master, Hazel could barely begin to imagine how it must feel.

'What will you do with him?'

'Nothing. Not tonight, anyway. First I must think about it. Why did he tell? Was it a mistake? Was it a moment of weakness? Was there some reason that he could not refuse?'

Was he just a selfish apprentice who couldn't keep his mouth shut? Poor Mr Volio, thought Hazel. He'll probably just make the apprentice eat a hundred éclairs as a punishment.

'Anyway,' said Mr Volio, suddenly clapping his hands,

'first there's something else we have to take care of: it's because of me you're not allowed to march, so now it's up to *me* to make sure you can!'

'I suppose we'll have to talk to Mr Winkel.'

'Yes, Mr Winkel. Come on, Hazel, he's probably still in his shop.'

'There's something else first, Mr Volio. You see, the tower's too tall.'

'The tower?'

'The tower of the Moodey Building that we're making. It's too tall and the wind's going to blow it over. That's how all this trouble started.'

'Really?' said Mr Volio, trying to understand. 'You have a tower and it's too tall, because—'

'Because of the wind! There's someone you should talk to, Mr Volio. Do you know a boy called the Yak?'

'The Yak?' said Mr Volio, shaking his head. Where did she learn these things? First the tower and now this boy called the Yak: what kind of a name was this?

'He's really called Yakov, but only his mother calls him that. The Yak can tell you why the tower's too tall.'

'Well, bring him down,' said Mr Volio.

'It would probably be easier if we went to see him.'

'Is he far away?'

'Oh, no,' said Hazel. 'He's right above our heads.'

Mr Volio looked up at the ceiling. Hazel looked up as well.

The door of the bakery opened.

'What are you looking for? Don't tell me there are spiders again!' It was young Mrs Volio. 'If those boys haven't cleared the cobwebs away I'll make them eat a pound of dough each, without any sugar!'

Mr Volio stood up. 'Teresa, I have something to tell you. Hazel Green didn't tell about the Chocolate Dippers.'

'Well, it's about time you realised, Stephen. How often did I tell you?' Mrs Volio gazed warmly at Hazel. 'So who was it? Do we know?'

'We're not quite sure yet,' said Mr Volio, winking at Hazel.

'That's right, Mrs Volio, we're not *quite* sure.'

'Well, I'm sure we'll find out.'

'Oh, yes, I'm sure we will,' said Mr Volio. 'Come on, Hazel, we'd better go.'

'Go? It's almost time to start work,' said Mrs Volio, moistening a handkerchief and dabbing at the flour on Mr Volio's face.

'We have to see someone first, Teresa.'

'Who?'

'A boy called the Yak,' said Mr Volio.

'He lives on top of the spiders,' added Hazel as she followed Mr Volio out.

16

It turned out that mathematicians did like cakes, at least, that's what it looked like, because Mr Volio brought a whole boxful with him, and they sat in the front room of the Yak's apartment, where there were enough sofas and armchairs for thirty people, and ate them. Even the

Yak's mother came in and had a pastry, dressed in a butterscotch coloured gown with crimson shoes. Her hair was black and her brooch was bronze. Mr Volio thought she looked lovely and told her so, but she simply

smiled and nodded, as if people often told her that she looked lovely and she hardly noticed any more. She didn't stay for long. As for the Yak, he quickly finished one cake and was soon reaching for a second.

Mr Volio watched him with satisfaction. There was nothing he liked more than seeing someone enjoying his cakes. It made all the hours of hard work, the heat of the oven, the clouds of flour, the pounding of the dough, worthwhile.

'I understand you like pretzels as well,' said Mr Volio eventually.

'Yes,' said the Yak, 'if they're fresh.'

'Mine are always fresh. You should come into the shop one day, Yakov, and I'll give you one.'

The Yak glanced at Hazel. Hazel shrugged. There were better things than pretzels in Mr Volio's shop!

Mr Volio looked around. He glanced over all the armchairs and sofas.

'Do a lot of people come to visit here?' he asked.

'No,' said the Yak.

'Oh,' said Mr Volio. 'Well, a lot of people *could* come here. They'd be very comfortable.'

'Not all the chairs are comfortable,' replied the Yak. 'Some of them could do with new springs.'

'Really?' said Mr Volio.

'Yes. Like that one over there,' said the Yak, pointing to an armchair in the corner. 'You wouldn't be comfortable in that one. I think we should throw it out.'

'Why don't you?' asked Hazel.

The Yak didn't say. He pursed his lips and gazed quizzically at the box of cakes on the table. Oh, no, thought Hazel, he's going to start thinking about a mathematical problem again. It was like a disease, the way that happened to the Yak when he was meant to be concentrating on other things. Somebody better say something soon, thought Hazel, or he'll be gone!

'Well, Yakov,' said Mr Volio, 'I understand the tower is too tall.'

The Yak looked up with a start. 'Yes,' he said.

'Why?'

'It's the height . . .'

Hazel grinned. But it wasn't meant to be a joke.

'In relation to the width,' the Yak added.

'I see,' said Mr Volio.

'Yakov can prove it,' said Hazel.

'Really?'

The Yak nodded. 'I showed Hazel already.'

'Can you show me?' said Mr Volio.

'If you like. It's not a very difficult proof.'

The Yak got up and left the room.

'He likes to prove by subtraction,' said Hazel while he was out. 'It's the most elegant way.'

The Yak came back with some paper. He sat down and leaned forward over the table, and soon he was scribbling the equations. When he was finished, he handed the page to Mr Volio.

Mr Volio held the sheet gingerly. He stared at the figures as if he thought they were going to jump up and bite him.

'Both sides?' he whispered to Hazel.

Hazel nodded. 'But this one's the most important,' she said, pointing to the side with the equations which ended with 3.7. 'That's the maximum height of the tower. Not a centimetre taller.'

Mr Volio looked up at the Yak. 'And you're sure about this?'

'There's no place for uncertainty in mathematics, Mr Volio,' said the Yak. 'Something's either right or it isn't.'

Mr Volio glanced at Hazel.

'Don't worry. He's sure, Mr Volio.'

'But if the tower fell over, that would be a disaster!' exclaimed Mr Volio.

'A catastrophe,' said Hazel.

'An unfortunate incident,' said the Yak.

'We can't let it happen.' Mr Volio jumped up. 'Come on, Hazel. Mr Winkel must be told!'

'Now?'

'Why not? Today is better than tomorrow.'

Hazel grinned. She jumped up as well.

'Aren't you coming, Yakov?' said Mr Volio.

The Yak shook his head. Why did people always want

someone to come along and talk, when the truth was written perfectly clearly in front of them? He picked up the paper and handed it to Mr Volio.

'That's all you need,' he said.

Hazel sighed. 'Come on, Mr Volio. Yakov's right.'

Mr Volio hesitated. 'Well, say goodbye to your mother for me,' he said eventually.

'All right,' said the Yak, but his tone was already far away, and he was staring at the cakes again, and Hazel couldn't tell if he was dropping deep into the tangle of a mathematical problem or just trying to decide which one he should try next.

'That's funny,' said Mr Volio, glancing at his watch, 'I wonder where Mr Winkel is. He's usually open for another twenty minutes at least.'

They were on the pavement in front of the leather goods shop. Hazel peered in through the window, trying to see past the big saddle in the centre. It was dark inside, but it always looked dark in there, even when the shop was open. Yet it was definitely closed. The door

was locked, and Mr Winkel's 'Closed' sign was in the window amongst a display of wallets and doeskin keycases.

'Where could he have gone?' murmured Mr Volio.

'Mr McCulloch's gone as well,' said Hazel, noticing that the door to the barber's shop was closed.

'That *is* strange,' said Mr Volio. 'He's always open late. Only last week he trimmed my moustache for me, and it must have been an hour later than it is now.'

Hazel peered at Mr Volio curiously. Trimmed his moustache? What a strange thing for a person to do. 'How often do you have to trim your moustache, Mr Volio?' she asked.

'Well, I suppose every couple of weeks. I hadn't really thought about it.'

So he *was* serious. He really did have to trim his moustache! Somehow it had never occurred to Hazel that you would have to trim a moustache. She had always thought they were more like . . . eyebrows. Or eyelashes. You didn't have to trim eyelashes, did you?

'How do you know when to trim it?'

Mr Volio was glancing at his watch again. 'What was that, Hazel? Oh, it just gets too long. Come on, we've got other things to think about.'

But this was really interesting! 'How do you know when it gets too long?'

Mr Volio scratched his head. 'There are two ways,

Hazel. The first, is that Mrs Volio tells me. And the second, is that it gets in my soup!'

Hazel laughed. 'In your soup?'

'When I put my spoon in my mouth. But I don't mind that too much. In fact, it gives you something to lick if you get hungry later. No, the first way is the one I can't ignore. If Teresa tells me it's too long, there's no choice: it needs a trim!'

'Yes, I suppose that's so,' said Hazel, wondering what it must be like to have a big handlebar moustache above your lip, and she rubbed her finger under her nose, as if that might show her.

'Well, it looks like we'll have to come back tomorrow,' said Mr Volio. He folded the paper with the Yak's proof and put it in his pocket. They turned and began to walk back towards his bakery.

'It's very strange that Mr McCulloch wasn't there either,' said Hazel.

'Yes, it is strange.'

'I wonder if they could have gone somewhere together.'

'Where would they go?' said Mr Volio.

Hazel shrugged. She looked into Mrs Gluck's window as they passed her shop. Mrs Gluck was just switching off the light in her workroom. Hazel waved at her.

'Perhaps they went to have a coffee at the *Vienna*,' said Hazel.

'Mr Winkel never goes there,' said Mr Volio.

'No, Mr Volio. He *nevver* goes there.'

'That's what I said.'

'No it isn't.'

Mr Volio frowned. 'Hazel Green, sometimes I don't—'

Mr Volio stopped. There was a noise coming from somewhere.

'Do you hear something, Hazel?'

Hazel nodded. They were standing near the entrance to the Moodey Building. It sounded as if people were cheering and clapping inside.

Suddenly the noise ceased. There was silence, the kind of silence that's too deep, as if there's something wrong. It couldn't have lasted for more than half a minute, but it seemed much longer. And then it ended . . . with a big, resounding crash.

17

Something very unusual had taken place behind the Coughlins' fruit shop that afternoon. It involved a door, which was at the very end of the dark passage that led past the Coughlins' three storerooms, a door that had not been opened for years. Perhaps it was originally intended as a way for people to bring goods into the storerooms at the back of the shop, but the Coughlins had not used it even once in all the time that they had owned the shop, and it was doubtful that the Biffetts, who had the shop before them, had ever used it either. They brought their goods in through the front of the shop. The problem with the door at the back was that it was not really a very practical way to bring goods in, for one simple reason: it opened onto the courtyard.

But that afternoon, as Mr Volio and Hazel and the Yak were sitting in the front room of the Yak's apartment, Mr Coughlin was struggling to get the door open. The big, old-fashioned key, that had rested untouched in a drawer for at least twenty years, caught in the rusty lock and wouldn't turn until half a can of oil had been poured into the keyhole to lubricate it. Then the door handle, which had grown stiff with age, refused to budge until it was coaxed down millimetre by millimetre. And finally the hinges, rusty, stiff and screechy, required oiling and coaxing, coaxing and oiling, before the door began to open. Mr Coughlin worked and worked at it. Finally, after almost an hour, the hinges began to turn. A crack appeared. The hinges turned further—and daylight poured into the passage for the first time in decades.

The door stood open. Mr Coughlin crossed his tired arms in satisfaction. He was not alone. In fact, there was a whole crowd watching him. Leon Davis was there, and Mandy Furstow, and Cobbler, Marcus Bunn, Sophie Wigg, Hamish Rae, Alli Reddick, Abby Simpkin, Paul Boone and of course Robert Fischer, who jumped around in excitement like an orang-utan when he saw the door open. And not only that, Mr McCulloch was there, and Mr Winkel as well.

But it wasn't the door that they were interested in. It was something else that made everyone tingle with excitement—everyone except Mr Winkel, and even he may have felt a shiver of anticipation.

'I think it will just fit through,' said Mr Coughlin.

The others nodded. Sophie Wigg had already measured it to make sure.

'Well, what are we waiting for?' said Mr McCulloch.

'Nothing!' shouted Leon Davis, and he turned around to the others. 'Ready?'

'Yes!'

They spread out along the passage. Everyone crouched. Between them, along the floor in the corridor, the

Moodey tower rested on its side.

'All right, on the count of three. One . . . two . . . *three*!'

Everyone heaved. In one smooth movement, they

lifted the construction off the ground. The Moodey
tower was complete, and they were about to take it out
into the courtyard and stand it upright for the first time.

There was hardly ever any wind in the courtyard of the
Moodey Building. The enormous height of the walls
protected it on all sides, as if it were the bottom of a vast
well. High above, storms might rage across the city,
but barely a puff would be felt below. Occasionally,
of course, a breath of wind did make it down there.
It would come swooping and swirling from above,
bouncing off the walls and whipping round and round
like a whirlpool, and when it reached the bottom it would
lift any bits of paper that were on the ground and throw

them flipping and flapping into the air, until, having nowhere else to go, it died out against the walls of the ground floor. Then the bits of paper would fall back on the cobblestones of the yard, and lie there until another breath of wind found its way down to jitter and jolt them, or until Mr Egozian, the caretaker, came out to take them away.

Just what it was that would send a particular puff of wind, at a particular time, swirling down the middle of the Moodey Building and into the courtyard was difficult to say. Perhaps a geographer or an experienced meteorologist could have explained the reasons. But none of the people who came out into the courtyard that day, when Mr Coughlin pushed open the door at the back of his shop and they brought the tower out into the open for the first time, was a geographer or a meteorologist, and none of them could have told you. As far as *they* were concerned, it was just a matter of luck.

Standing the tower upright turned out to be remarkably easy. That was the part that everyone had been worried about. Would they be able to swing it up? Would it crack in the middle as they hoisted it? But it all went like clockwork. Marcus Bunn and Mandy Furstow crouched at its foot and anchored it, to prevent it slipping, and the others went to the top end and began to lift. They raised it above their heads and then they walked towards Marcus and Mandy, still pushing upwards, so the angle of the tower increased. Finally it was almost vertical, and Mr

McCulloch helped steady it into position. Then, on a signal from Leon Davis, they all let go and stepped backwards. Last of all Mr McCulloch moved away.

And there it was, a replica of the Moodey Building, as they had barely dared to imagine it.

At first everyone just stared, too fascinated to say anything. Each shop was shown on the ground floor, every storey and window was visible. It rose high above their heads, and when they looked up to follow it to the top, there behind it were the windows of the real Moodey Building, gazing down at this perfect copy of itself. And it *was* perfect, or at least it looked like it. Starting off with a jumble of old boxes and nails and paint in the dim light of the Coughlins' storeroom, it had been hard to believe that one day the tower would stand tall and proud in the sunlight, as it was standing today in front of their eyes.

Then someone cheered. It just came out. It might have been Hamish Rae, it might have been Sophie Wigg. Then someone else joined in. And others. Suddenly *everyone* was cheering and clapping. Cobbler put his fingers in his mouth and produced an ear-splitting whistle. Hamish Rae roared and slapped his thighs and stamped his feet, making as much noise as he could. Sophie Wigg yelled and jumped from one foot to the other, waving her arms above her head. Susie Bunn started turning cartwheels. Everyone else was jumping and shouting. Robert Fischer cavorted around the tower four times and almost collided with Susie as she somersaulted past him, before running off to find a ladder so he could take his seat on the top.

Maybe it was the clapping and the cheering that did it. Maybe it set up some kind of vibration in the air, which sucked down a tiny puff of a breeze that happened to be passing above them across the city. A geographer or meteorologist would have been able to say. Anyway, whatever the reason, it was just at that minute that a breath of wind *was* sucked out of the sky into the vast well of the Moodey Building. Suddenly it was bouncing from side to side off the walls and swirling down at a dizzying pace towards the courtyard. It took only seconds to reach the bottom. But even then it was only a gentle puff of wind, not much stronger than someone blowing against your cheek.

An old bus ticket rose off the cobblestones and jiggled in the air. Still the cheering went on. No one noticed. Even Mr Winkel was clapping.

But even as they cheered, there were the first puzzled looks. People blinked. What was that they had just seen? Had the tower rocked?

It *had* rocked. Now it was rocking again!

The cheering grew quieter. The tower rocked: one way, then the other.

There was one last whoop from Hamish Rae. Then he was quiet as well. Now there was silence, complete silence. The tower was really wobbling. It lurched from side to side, leaning further each time than the time before.

Sometimes, when something really unexpected happens, people freeze. Later, they know what they should have done, but for some reason no one moves at the time. In the courtyard of the Moodey Building, that was what was happening.

Everyone watched in horror, paralysed. The tower could have been saved if only someone, one person, perhaps two, had run forwards to steady it. But no one moved.

Already the wind was dying down, but it was too late. Before their eyes, the tower rocked one last time . . . teetered . . . and fell with an enormous crash.

18

The tower was lying on
the ground in two pieces.
It had cracked about a
metre from the end. The
top three storeys of the
Moodey Building lay by
themselves, as if they had
decided to split off and
start an apartment block
of their own.

Hazel Green and Mr
Volio, who had run into the courtyard as soon as they
heard the crash, found the others still gazing at the
pieces, speechless, as if they couldn't quite believe what
they had just seen—that a tiny puff of wind had rocked
and broken the tower—as if in reality it were still
standing upright and proud and all of this falling and
cracking were just a bad dream from which everyone, in
a moment, would awaken.

But no one did awake from the dream, because it was
not a dream at all, as the Yak could have told them even
before it had happened.

'Well . . .' said Mr Volio.

Mr Winkel looked around sharply. 'Stephen? Is that

all you can say: Well!'

'It was bound to happen,' said Mr Volio.

'Was it really? Bound to happen?' Now Mr Winkel noticed Hazel. 'You! You always know when to turn up. I suppose you'll say it was bound to happen as well.'

'Of course,' said Hazel. 'It was perfectly obvious.'

'Perfectly ob . . . Perfect . . . Perfectly obvi . . .' spluttered Mr Winkel, arching his eyebrows and bulging his eyes and stretching his neck so much that the words simply couldn't get out.

'Don't listen to her,' cried Leon Davis, 'you can't believe anything she says!'

'Really?' said Hazel. 'And what about you?'

'Me?'

'You! Don't tell me you're going to pretend you didn't know.'

'Know what?'

Hazel rolled her eyes. He *was* going to pretend. Oh, well, she thought, sighing, I'll just have to tell everyone for him. 'Of course he knew. We all knew.'

'Knew what?' demanded Mr Winkel.

'Yes, what?' said Mr McCulloch.

'That the tower was going to—'

'We didn't! We didn't,' shouted Leon Davis.

'Know what?' said Mr Winkel.

'Nothing! We didn't know anything.'

'Nothing?'

'Nothing!' shouted Leon, and the others were shouting as well.

Really, thought Hazel.

'Silence!' cried Mr Winkel. 'Silence! Silence! Si-*lence*!'

There was silence. Mr Winkel waited for a moment. Then he turned to Leon Davis. 'And what, exactly, is this thing you *didn't* know?'

'Nothing, really,' muttered Leon Davis.

'Nothing? Perhaps I should ask Hazel Green.'

Go on, thought Hazel.

'Well?'

Leon Davis shuffled his feet. He was a very unpredictable boy. Sometimes he could be so quiet, yet at other times you just couldn't stop him talking!

'Well?'

'That it was going to fall.'

'*What* . . .' demanded Mr Winkel, cupping a hand to his ear, 'did you say?'

'That it was going to fall.' Leon glanced back down at his feet. 'It was going to be too tall and the wind would knock it over.'

Mr Winkel folded his arms across his chest. He sent a stinging glance at Mr McCulloch, as if to say that all of this was his fault, and none of it would have happened if only he had listened to him, Mr Winkel, at the beginning. Children in parades meant only one thing— trouble!

'You mean you knew this all along, Leon?' inquired Mr McCulloch.

'Not really,' said Leon, squirming, and the others murmured as well, 'not really' or 'kind of' or 'maybe'.

But Mr McCulloch, even though he wanted to be as helpful as possible, just didn't understand how you could 'kind of' or 'not really' know something, and Hazel was quite interested to find out as well.

'It was only the Yak who said so,' said Leon, hoping that would make it clear.

'The Yak?' said Mr Winkel, slapping a hand to his forehead despairingly. The more you talked to these children, the less you understood.

'Yakov Plonsk,' said Leon. 'Yakov had a theory—'

'It wasn't a theory. It was a proof!' corrected Hazel.

'All right, a proof,' Leon admitted grudgingly. 'But who can understand his proofs?'

'What difference does it make if you can't understand them?'

'Neither can you!'

'So?'

'Enough!' shouted Mr Winkel, who still had his hand on his forehead. Maybe he was getting a headache, thought Hazel.

'I think I can help,' said Mr Volio, taking the Yak's proof out of his pocket and handing the paper to Mr Winkel.

'Oh, yes,' said Mr Winkel, gazing at the lines of complicated equations, 'this *really* helps.'

'You see,' said Leon, 'who can understand it?'

Mr Winkel handed the paper back to Mr Volio. 'What does it mean, Stephen?'

'That the tower would fall if the wind was stronger than 4.8 kilometres per hour.'

'I see,' said Mr Winkel. He looked at the broken tower on the ground in front of him. 'Well, it certainly did.'

Hazel threw a triumphant glance at Leon Davis. But when she looked back at Mr Winkel, she found that something horrible had happened: Mr Winkel, who was still surveying the fallen tower, didn't look as if he had a headache any more, in fact, there was an unmistakable look of satisfaction under his bushy eyebrows, just the kind of look that an eagle would have, Hazel imagined, when it had spotted its prey and was about to swoop.

'It certainly did fall. Well, it can't be helped. I suppose there won't be any children marching on Frogg Day after all. What a shame,' Mr Winkel said, in a tone that sounded as if it were not a shame at all.

Hazel frowned. No children marching on Frogg Day? That wasn't the plan. That wasn't what was meant to happen!

'Coming, Bert?' said Mr Winkel, and he turned to go.

Hazel grabbed Mr Volio's sleeve. *'The other side, Mr Volio,'* she whispered, *'the other side.'*

'What other side?'

'Mr Winkel!' cried Hazel.

Mr Winkel stopped in front of the exit from the courtyard. Very slowly, he turned around.

'What?'

'There's more, Mr Winkel.'

Mr Winkel sighed. 'With you, Hazel Green, there's always more.'

Hazel pushed Mr Volio forwards. *'Show him the other side of the paper,'* she whispered urgently.

'Here,' said Mr Volio, who had forgotten what the Yak's second proof showed, 'have a look at the other side, Arthur.'

'Why?'

'Well . . . you'll understand when you see it.'

But the second side of the Yak's equations was no more comprehensible than the first. Mr Winkel glanced at the paper and looked back questioningly at Mr Volio.

'The height,' whispered Hazel.

'The height, Arthur.'

'3.7 metres.'

'3.7 metres.'

'What is?'

'The tower won't fall if the height isn't more than 3.7 metres,' said Hazel. 'The Yak proved it.'

Mr Winkel sighed. This *Yak* again. Did the girl think she could talk to animals now?

'The boy did prove it,' said Mr Volio.

Mr Winkel shrugged. 'He could be wrong. He's just a boy, isn't he?'

He wasn't *just* a boy. 'He's a mathematician!' cried Hazel.

'Arthur,' said Mr McCulloch, 'the boy *was* right the first time.'

Mr Winkel gave the paper back to Mr Volio. 'So?'

'So perhaps they could march after all.'

Mr Winkel laughed. None of the children had ever seen him laugh before, and it was not a pleasant sight. 'The march is *four* days away. Do you really think they can build another tower in that time?' Mr Winkel laughed again, as if he really couldn't stop himself.

'Yes,' said Hazel.

Mr Winkel ignored her. Perhaps if he ignored her everyone else would as well.

'You see, Mr Winkel, we don't really need to build another tower. We can use the one we have.'

'But it's broken!' cried Mr Winkel in exasperation. 'Can't you see that?'

'Even the long piece is still too tall, Mr Winkel. We just have to cut it back a bit. We can easily do that in four days.'

Mr Winkel's hand was on his forehead again. His headaches seemed to come and go very quickly.

'I know you'll be pleased, Mr Winkel. Think how

disappointed you'll be if none of the children march.'

For a moment Mr Winkel was silent. Then he shook his head in despair and groaned.

'Good,' said Mr McCulloch, 'that's settled. We just have to cut the tower down and then everything can go ahead as planned.'

'Excellent!' said Hazel Green. She grinned at Leon Davis, who was watching her sullenly.

'Wait a minute!' said Mr Winkel, wagging a finger. 'Wait just a minute. Not you, Hazel Green. You're not marching, remember?'

'But—'

'Oh, no. *You* . . . are out!'

Now Leon Davis grinned. 'Out,' he whispered.

'No, Arthur,' said Mr Volio.

Mr Winkel looked at him in surprise. 'But it was you who demanded it, Stephen!'

Mr Volio glanced at Hazel. 'Well, I was mistaken.'

Mr Winkel shrugged. 'It's too late now. Everyone knows Hazel Green is out. "Me or her", you said. Remember?'

'It's different now. Me *and* her,' said Mr Volio, putting his arm around Hazel's shoulder.

Mr Winkel snorted.

'Me *and* her, Arthur.'

'And me,' said Mr McCulloch, putting his arm around Hazel's other shoulder.

The three of them, Mr McCulloch, Hazel and Mr Volio, stood together, as one. Hazel didn't even need to look at Leon Davis to know that the grin had disappeared from his face.

Mr Winkel stared. His eyebrows had risen so high in disbelief that if they had gone any further they would have slipped right off the back of his head.

19

Four days wasn't much, but it was enough to cut down the tower and repaint the top and get it ready to stand again. Sophie Wigg's father brought his saw and did the cutting, and after that it didn't take long. Of course, the proportions were no longer quite right, and the building only had ten storeys instead of fourteen, so it wasn't a *perfect* copy of the Moodey Building any more, but it was still tall and imposing, and everyone would certainly still recognise it when it came down the street in the parade, and that was the most important thing.

'After all,' said Mrs Gluck, 'no one's going to count the number of storeys, are they?'

'No,' said Hazel.

'And if Robert Fischer is going to be sitting on it, well, that's already a difference. We don't have a great big Robert Fischer sitting on top of the real Moodey Building, do we?'

'No,' said Hazel.

'No, fortunately,' said Mrs Gluck, chuckling to herself. 'What do you call him, Hazel? Remind me.'

'An orang-utan.'

'That's right, an orang-utan,' said Mrs Gluck, still chuckling. 'Sometimes you really are terrible, Hazel.'

Good, thought Hazel. Everyone should be terrible sometimes.

Mrs Gluck continued working. It was the day before Frogg Day and she had *hundreds* of orders to prepare. Tomorrow there would be banquets and parties all over the city, and everyone wanted spectacular arrangements of flowers to brighten up the festivities. The whole workroom was a mass of orange, which was the colour of Frogg Day. In the march, everyone wore orange sashes across their chests. Each of Mrs Gluck's bouquets had at least one orange flower at its centre. Some people had ordered arrangements of nothing *but* orange, and Mrs Gluck had created fantastic combinations of orange roses, lilies, tulips and carnations, dark oranges and light oranges, flat oranges and crinkly oranges, so many oranges and so many textures that even these arrangements looked like whole tapestries of colour in themselves. They stood all around her in the workroom, waiting to be delivered. These creations were the greatest challenge and Mrs Gluck was famous for the way she was able to construct dazzling Frogg Day displays out of a single colour.

Suddenly Mrs Gluck laughed, still thinking about orang-utans. 'What do you think it would look like, if we *did* have a gigantic orang-utan on top of the Moodey Building?' she said.

'Ugly,' said Hazel.

'Why?'

'Because it would remind me of Robert Fischer all the time!'

Mrs Gluck laughed again, and told Hazel that she was terrible, but Hazel didn't think she really was being terrible at this particular point, because it really would be an ugly thing if she had to be reminded of Robert Fischer each time she looked up at the building in which she lived. It was bad enough to be reminded of him each time he pranced around and hit himself in the back of the head with his own satchel on the way to school.

'Well, I'm glad you're marching,' said Mrs Gluck. 'Of course, I knew you would. I never doubted you'd find a way in the end.' She was wrapping a length of twine around the stems of an arrangement that she had just completed. Hazel watched her strong hands twisting the twine tight. The cords of muscle in Mrs Gluck's wrists tensed and pulled. 'What about Yakov, is he marching with you?' she said as she knotted the twine.

'Yakov marching?' Hazel was surprised. What a strange idea! 'No, I don't think so.'

'Why not?'

Why not? Hazel frowned. 'Well, mathematicians don't—'

'Nonsense, Hazel. Have you asked him?'

'Mathematicians really are quite strange, Mrs Gluck.

You have to understand that.'

Mrs Gluck didn't reply. She set the finished arrangement aside. She paused to glance at Hazel, raising one eyebrow sceptically. Then she went to gather the flowers for the next order.

But they really *are* strange, Mrs Gluck, thought Hazel. The Yak . . . who could imagine him marching with a bunch of other kids and an orange sash across his chest?

Hazel walked back towards the Moodey Building entrance, past the other shops on the ground floor. Light spilled out from them into the darkening street and they were all busy. Everyone was getting ready for Frogg Day. Mr Petrusca was filleting great piles of fish for customers who were having lunch parties tomorrow. The queue from the McCulloch fruit shop stretched into the street. People were fighting over the last pickled cucumber in the Frengels' delicatessen. Both the bakeries of Mr Volio and Mr Murray were packed with people picking up cakes. Everything was noisy and bright, lively and warm. Hazel could have walked up and down, up and down, over and over again, just gazing at everyone and everything and all the faces and all the hands reaching over counters to take bags, packets and parcels from the shopkeepers. In fact, she did walk up and down a few times, and once she caught the eye of Mr Petrusca, who smiled but couldn't spare her a glance of more than a second, so many customers were still clamouring and so many fish did he still have to fillet.

She came across Marcus Bunn. He was peering into the butcher's shop. His nose was pressed up against the window.

'What are you looking at?' said Hazel.

Marcus jumped in fright. When he saw who it was, he pointed at one of the trays in the butcher's display.

'Tongues?' said Hazel.

The tongues were long and grey, and they had a dull surface that looked like rubber.

'What are *you* doing?' said Marcus.

'Just walking.'

Marcus nodded. 'My mother's got my sash ready,' he said. 'She made one for Mandy as well.'

'Why couldn't Mandy's mother make one?' asked Hazel.

Marcus shrugged. He looked back at the butcher's window. 'She would have made one for you as well, if you'd asked.'

Hazel already had a sash. 'What is your mother, Marcus, the neighbourhood sash maker?'

'Very funny.'

Hazel looked into the butcher's window as well. There was a sheep's head towards the back of the display and she gazed at its big, staring eyes.

'What are you going to do now?' asked Marcus.

'Don't know. Maybe I'll go home.'

Marcus hesitated. He glanced at Hazel from behind his spectacles. It was a long time since he had gone to Mrs Gluck's workroom with her. It was a long time since he had gone anywhere with Hazel.

Hazel waited for him to speak. But in the end all he said was: 'Eight o'clock tomorrow morning?'

'That's right. Eight o'clock. Everyone has to be in front of the building. If you're late they won't let you march.'

'I won't be late.'

'Good,' Hazel turned. 'Don't eat too many tongues!' she cried over her shoulder, as she mixed into the crowd of people moving along the pavements.

Marcus was always late for things. But he would have to be there at eight o'clock in the morning. It would take an hour just to reach the square where the march started, and they had to take the Moodey tower with them. Mr Winkel had set the time and even Mr McCulloch agreed. Eight o'clock and not a minute later. Everyone who was going to march had to be there.

Hazel walked back along the pavement. When she went past the flower shop, she could see that the light in the workroom was still on. Mrs Gluck would probably be working until midnight.

No, Mrs Gluck just didn't understand about the Yak, she thought. After all, she didn't know a single mathematician. You had to know a mathematician to understand what they were really like.

Hazel turned and went back into the Moodey Building. She pressed the button for the elevator. It took a while to arrive. He won't want to march, it's as simple as that, she told herself over and over as she waited. What did Mrs Gluck know? He'd just laugh. What was the point of asking him?

But when the elevator finally arrived, and she got in, it wasn't the button for the twelfth floor, where she lived, that she pressed. Somehow she ended up making another stop first.

20

The Yak's mother was wearing a ruby-coloured gown with indigo shoes. Her brooch was platinum and her hair was chestnut.

'Is Yakov in?' said Hazel.

'Of course,' said the Yak's mother, and she turned to go and get him.

This time Hazel followed her. She didn't wait in the hallway with all the furniture. She didn't want to go and sit in the big room that was cluttered with sofas. The Yak's mother didn't even realise she was behind her. When she opened the Yak's door, Hazel was already peering in under her elbow.

'Yakov . . .' said the Yak's mother.

'Hello,' said Hazel.

The Yak's mother looked down in surprise, but Hazel was already inside the room. The Yak, who had been leaning back in his chair with his head turned up and his eyes closed, looked around with a start. But Hazel knew he hadn't been asleep.

'You ought to go out in the fresh air and eat a pretzel when you're tying to solve a problem,' said Hazel.

'Yes, Yakov,' said the Yak's mother, without knowing what Hazel was talking about. 'That sounds like a very good idea. Fresh air is good for you.'

Hazel sat down on the end of the Yak's bed.

'Yes. Fresh air. That's a very good idea. Just what he needs . . .' the Yak's mother was saying to herself. And a moment later she was gone.

Hazel looked around at the Yak's room. It was the neatest room she had ever seen. There was none of the clutter that occupied the rest of the apartment. There was a big desk, and there wasn't very much on it, just a few pages and a large pile of scrap paper for scribbling. There was a set of bookshelves with a lot of books tidily arranged. There was a window. In front of it was a music

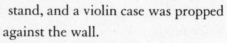 stand, and a violin case was propped against the wall.

'Do you play it?' asked Hazel.

The Yak looked as if he didn't really want to answer. 'Yes,' he said eventually.

'A lot?' said Hazel.

The Yak shrugged.

'Is that why you never go outside?'

'Of course I go outside.'

'Yes, to go to school.' Hazel laughed. 'And if you're wearing a balaclava!'

The Yak didn't want to laugh, Hazel could see that. She waited. In the end he couldn't help grinning. His pointy face creased. Hazel laughed again. Why was the Yak so different? Why didn't he behave like everybody *else? She* wouldn't like to be that way. A week of being kept out of everything, of walking to school by herself and having to listen to everyone else talking about what was going on, had been enough. But the Yak lived like that all the time!

'Why do you play the violin?' asked Hazel suddenly.

The Yak frowned. Why? No one ever asked why. Most people asked whether he played well. 'I like to, I suppose.'

'But why do you like to?'

The Yak frowned. 'Because . . . music has order.'

'Order?'

The Yak nodded.

Hazel thought about that. Order. Was that a good thing? She wasn't sure. She had never thought about it before. *Order.* No, she didn't think she liked too much order.

'I like confusion,' she decided.

The Yak looked interested. 'Confusion? Why?'

'I don't know,' said Hazel. Suddenly she jumped up and went over to the window. It looked down on the courtyard. 'Is this where you saw Mr Volio say that I told about the Chocolate Dippers?'

'Yes,' said the Yak from behind her.

'Why did you watch?'

There was no reply.

'There was a lot of confusion *that* day!' said Hazel, laughing.

The Yak laughed as well.

Hazel sat down on the bed again. 'Tell me about order,' she said.

'What do you mean?'

'Well, what's so good about it?'

'The world is based on order,' said the Yak. 'The physical forces that make things happen, the logic of thought, the sequence of—'

'No, it isn't!' said Hazel. 'I've never heard such nonsense. The world is a great big soup and everything is mixed up in it.'

The Yak stared. 'A *soup*?'

Hazel nodded. That's exactly what it was, a soup. And not a very clear soup. Not a broth, that was for sure. A thick, rich, chunky, swirly, mixed up soup with a great big dollop of cream added just to confuse everything even more.

'I don't think it's a soup,' said the Yak.

'What do you think it is? An egg?'

'No, not an egg.' The Yak thought.

'A bean?'

'No.'

'A marble cake?'

'No!'

'What, then?'

'Let me think,' said the Yak, and that is what he started to do. It went on for a long time.

'A stuffed pepper?'

'No. I'll tell you what it is: a drop of honey.'

'And I suppose you're swimming in it!'

'No one's swimming in it. A *perfectly* formed drop. With a fine tip and an absolutely spherical body. Completely symmetrical. Perfectly smooth. And absolutely translucent, so you can see through to its very centre from every side without a single disruption.'

Hazel grimaced. That wasn't *her* world. She didn't live in an *absolutely perfect* drop of honey. If she did, it wouldn't stay perfect for long! No, she lived in a soup, and you could never tell what chunk you were going to bump into next.

The Yak leaned back in his chair, looking very pleased with himself.

'Well, I'm glad you're wrong,' said Hazel.

'I'm not wrong,' said the Yak.

'And I suppose mathematics is part of the order in the world?'

The Yak smiled his pointy grin. 'It *is* the order in the world.'

Hazel snorted. 'What, two plus two equals four? What kind of a great order is that?'

'Yes, even that,' said the Yak. 'Even the simplest thing, like two plus two equals four.'

Hazel hadn't expected that. She had expected the Yak to laugh at two plus two equals four and say that was just child's play, not real mathematics, and that *real* mathematics was much more complicated.

'But even babies know that,' said Hazel.

'So?'

'Well, how important can it be?'

The Yak got up and pulled a book off the shelf. He opened it and put it in front of Hazel. 'Look. This is a whole book about something called Fermat's last theorem. It looks so simple, but it's the most difficult mathematical problem ever. People have tried to prove it for years. Look at it. Look how complicated it gets when you try to understand it.'

Hazel looked. The pages of the book were covered in thick text interrupted by equations. The text was rich in symbols. Hazel tried to read a paragraph and didn't understand the first line.

'Even I can't understand some of this,' said the Yak. 'Not yet. But . . .' He hesitated. Then he said: 'One day, I will prove Fermat's last theorem. The man who wrote this book thinks he's already done it, but I can do it better. I know I can, even if I have to write a whole new book of my own.'

Hazel looked up. There was a faraway gaze in the Yak's eyes. Then he suddenly realised that she was looking at him, and blinked, and began to blush.

'I sh . . . shouldn't have said that,' he stammered. 'I've never . . .'

He didn't finish the sentence. But he didn't have to.

'It's all right,' said Hazel, 'I won't tell.'

'Do you promise?'

'On my nose,' said Hazel, and she put a finger gravely on the tip of her nose.

The Yak grinned. 'They'd probably think up some other horrible name for me. They'd call me Fur Man or something.'

Hazel bit her lip. 'Yakov,' she said. 'I've got something to tell *you*.'

'What?'

Hazel hesitated. It wasn't too late to turn back—but she didn't. 'It's just . . . well, *I* made that name up.'

'Fur Man? I didn't even know people were calling me that.'

'No, not *Fur Man*. The Yak. Your name, the Yak.'

The Yak stared at her.

'Well, I mean, it *is* quite funny.'

Still the Yak stared.

'And, after all, they *are* quite nice animals. Although they do smell a bit.' Hazel tried to keep from laughing. 'And of course, they have fleas, but not too many.'

'You . . . ?'

Hazel nodded. 'I'm sorry. I wouldn't do it now.'

The Yak shook his head. 'You would.'

Hazel laughed again. 'You're right, I would. I wouldn't be able to help myself.'

The Yak reached out and took the book on Fermat from Hazel's hand. Silently, he put it back on the shelf.

'Yakov?'

'What?'

'I probably *would* do it now. But not for the same reason.'

'Not for the same reason? Well, that's nice to hear.'

'And I wouldn't tell anyone. It would just be a name that *I* would use for you.'

'Really? And what is the point of a name that only *you* would use for me? Who would you tell it to? When would you use it?'

'Yakov, when I first made it up, it was to make fun of you.'

'And now?'

Hazel crossed her arms. She bunched up her shoulders. Suddenly she felt embarrassed. Hazel Green hardly ever felt embarrassed. She knew what she wanted to say but she didn't know how to say it. She could feel herself going red. She hated going red, and as soon as she realised she was doing it, she always went even redder.

'Are you going to march tomorrow?' she blurted out suddenly, remembering why she had come to talk to the Yak in the first place.

The Yak stared at her. Slowly his lips curled in a grin.

'Because if you need a sash, I'm sure I can—'

Hazel stopped. The Yak was laughing, just as she knew he would. 'March?' he said eventually, 'why would I want to march?'

'It's your tower as much as anyone's. You're the one who worked out its height.'

'My tower? I don't want it. Believe me, I'm very happy for everyone to forget I had anything to do with it.'

'Have you ever thought you might have some fun? There'll be all sorts of people there, and everyone will be watching, and you can help push the tower, or march in front of it, and there'll be sandwiches, and . . .'

Hazel gave up. It was like talking to a brick wall. The Yak wasn't even listening.

'What *will* you do then? Work on your Fur Man's theorem?'

That woke him up: 'You said you'd never tell! You swore on your nose!'

'I can tell *you*!' cried Hazel. 'You're the one who told me!'

The Yak eyed her suspiciously.

'What *will* you do, Yakov? Prove something by subtraction? Play your violin?'

'Maybe. Why not?' He folded his arms. 'Maybe I will.'

'Don't do that, please. Don't play your violin.' Hazel couldn't bear the thought of it: the Yak up here all alone while the whole city was marching and celebrating. There was probably more confusion in the Frogg Day march than anywhere else in the whole world, but even the Yak's life wasn't always full of perfect order. Why wouldn't he admit it? After all, there was plenty of confusion when they set out to catch the apprentices. They didn't know *what* was going to happen. And the Yak didn't give up after the first day, he came back the next day and the day after. Maybe he even enjoyed it.

'What about when we caught the apprentices? You had fun then!'

The Yak didn't respond.

'Come and march with us tomorrow, Yakov.'

He shook his head.

'Then at least watch. Watch from your balcony.'

'Why should I? I've got better things to do.'

Hazel hesitated. She bit her lip. She knew she was going red again, but this time she didn't care.

'Because I want you to.'

'You want me to?' The Yak frowned. He didn't seem to know what to say. Then he shook his head. 'I've got better things to do.'

21

Hazel Green looked down from her balcony. It wasn't even six o'clock. It was earlier, much earlier than that. Far below, the street was almost empty. Two sweepers moved slowly along the pavements, like two black insects in the shadows. All over the city, other sweepers were doing the same. Today, the streets had to be spotless.

Far away, the edge of the sky was brightening. The sweepers disappeared round the corner. Now everything was completely still. The cold tiles and the chilly air made Hazel's skin tingle. Somewhere a bird twittered. Slowly, as she watched, the sky grew brighter. The street became clearer. Soon it would be filled with people, more people than ever before. But for now, the street, the whole city was *hers*, and there wasn't anyone else to share it with.

Mr Volio appeared on the pavement. He wasn't wearing his bakery clothes. He wore a white shirt, and a bright orange sash ran over the bulge of his belly. He threw his head back and let the sun warm his face. He stretched his arms out and turned from side to side, like a loose propeller in the wind. He opened his eyes. There was a big grin on his face.

'Hazel! Hazel Green!'

Hazel ran down the stairs. The bakery was silent and

empty, the oven was cold. No one had been working overnight. This morning, the shops would be closed. Mr Volio and Hazel sat down beside the kneading table and ate a Chocolate Dipper, the first on Frogg Day.

At ten past eight, an open truck set off from the Moodey Building. It belonged to Sophie Wigg's father, and in the back, attached to Cobbler's barrow, was the Moodey tower. Everyone had jumped up beside it. Only Marcus Bunn was late. He came tearing out of the Moodey Building just as the truck started up and everyone had to shout and shout to make Sophie Wigg's father stop to let

him on. Mr Winkel, who was following in his car, didn't look very happy, but even he couldn't prevent Marcus clambering aboard. Then they started off again, and this time they didn't stop until everyone jumped out at Victor Square, where the march was due to begin.

The square was boiling over with activity. There were people with orange sashes everywhere. The air crackled with trumpet calls and drum rolls and flute trills. Bands were warming up, acrobats were practising, marching leaders were tossing their batons. Every minute a truck arrived and unloaded another squadron of marchers. A line of floats stood along one edge of the square, and along another side there was a row of tables with big steaming mugs of coffee and thick pieces of bread covered with butter and jam for anyone to take. Even before they had finished rolling the Moodey tower down a pair of planks from the truck, Robert Fischer and Hamish Rae had run across to the tables and were wolfing down the bread.

There was so much to see in the square that they hardly knew where to begin. Robert Fischer, still gobbling his bread, stood gaping at the acrobats, while Mandy Furstow dragged Marcus Bunn over to listen to the bands. And then there were the floats to look at: a gigantic pineapple from the market traders, a sailing ship on wheels from the navy, an enormous flashing lightbulb from the electricity company. The watch-makers' guild had produced a huge clock with the face of Victor Frogg: his moustache was the hands. The zoo had sent a monkey dressed like a prince with an elephant to draw his wagon. As soon as Robert Fischer caught a glimpse of the monkey he ran across from the acrobats and stood there making faces at him. Paul Boone tried to get on the sailing ship. Sophie Wigg knocked on the pineapple to see if there was anyone inside. And all the time Mr Winkel ran up and down, trying to collect everybody and muttering under his breath about children and marches and the two not belonging together.

But gradually, almost before anyone noticed that it was happening, the confusion in the square began to disappear. The marching groups came together and started to get in line. One by one, the floats were taken from the side of the square to their places in the procession. The bands sent their last wave of trumpet calls and drum rolls into the air. The tables with the coffee and bread were cleared away.

Now the Moodey children themselves began to drift back towards their tower. Sophie Wigg's father and Mr McCulloch had put it in place near the head of the line. Big official cars, with little flags fluttering on their bonnets, were arriving in the square, and Government representatives were getting out, wearing bright orange sashes over their coats. They took their places at the very front of the procession.

Now there was a real hush. Everyone was waiting. All eyes were on the entrance to the square.

At last, a very grand car pulled up. The driver jumped out to open the back door. An old, frail lady emerged.

She looked around, surveying the procession. Then she turned and shuffled to the head of the parade.

Suddenly a wave of noise and activity broke out, as if everyone knew it was their last chance to get ready. The bands practised, the acrobats performed one last jump. Robert Fischer straightened his cape and clambered to the top of the Moodey tower where he was going to sit. Cobbler, Marcus Bunn and Mandy Furstow got ready to push the barrow. Sophie Wigg and Abby Simpkin got ready to steady it, the others stood in their positions around it. Hazel Green and Leon Davis took their places in front of the tower. Between them stood Mr Volio, holding up the Moodey Building banner.

Now, silence again.

Victor Frogg's granddaughter looked over her shoulder. She nodded, faced ahead once more—and took a step forward.

All together, the bands began to play. The Frogg March had begun.

Hazel had never known such noise. The streets were lined with people, on the pavements, on the balconies, on the rooftops. The cheering came from all sides. The marchers cheered in return. The music of the bands blared. Confetti and ticker tape rained down like snow. Flowers flew through the air. It was a blur, a wonderful, multicoloured, deafening blur of faces and noise, with snapshots that were suddenly frozen and clear and which would remain in Hazel's memory for years afterwards—like the image of Mr Volio straining with the banner and turning to smile at her for a second, or Robert Fischer on top of the tower waving his orang-utan arms above his head, or Hamish Rae clanging a pair of cymbals that he had secretly brought along—and then more blur, more faces, more noise.

And suddenly the noise was even louder.

They had just turned a corner. The Moodey Building rose ahead of them. And at the sight of the Moodey tower coming down the street towards it, signalling the arrival of its children, it was as if the building itself erupted in noise. Every balcony was packed, and every person on every balcony was cheering his head off. The children of the Moodey Building cheered back. They raised their arms, cheering and cheering until their voices were hoarse, each one searching for the faces of parents, friends, neighbours who were watching for them. Hazel looked as well. She saw Mrs Gluck on a first floor balcony, and almost imagined that she was wiping a tear from her eye. She saw Mr Petrusca on a second floor balcony, whose wife was marching in the adults' contingent behind her. Higher, much higher, she knew, on her own balcony on the twelfth floor, her parents, her aunties, her uncles and cousins, were watching. But before she looked all the way up, her eyes lingered for a moment, searching, wondering, looking for a balcony on the third floor.

Suddenly she heard no noise. Everything froze. For Hazel, there was no movement, no sound. It was as if everything else in the world had stopped and might never start again.

And then, just as his eyes found her, she found him as well.

He was there!

A big grin come across his pointy face. His arms rose, his mouth opened.

Then the huge noise all around deafened her once more.

And Hazel was cheering as well. Her arms were in the air, and she was shouting herself hoarse, just like every one of the Moodey children around her. And the Yak, high above, shouted and shouted in return.